ChangelingPress.com

Eagle/Cyrus Duet
A Bones MC Romance
Marteeka Karland

Eagle/Cyrus Duet
A Bones MC Romance
Marteeka Karland

All rights reserved.
Copyright ©2024 Marteeka Karland

ISBN: 978-1-60521-894-6

Publisher:
Changeling Press LLC
315 N. Centre St.
Martinsburg, WV 25404
ChangelingPress.com

Printed in the U.S.A.

Editor: Jean Cooper
Cover Artist: Marteeka Karland

The individual stories in this anthology have been previously released in E-Book format.

No part of this publication may be reproduced or shared by any electronic or mechanical means, including but not limited to reprinting, photocopying, or digital reproduction, without prior written permission from Changeling Press LLC.

This book contains sexually explicit scenes and adult language which some may find offensive and which is not appropriate for a young audience. Changeling Press books are for sale to adults, only, as defined by the laws of the country in which you made your purchase.

Table of Contents

Eagle (Iron Tzars MC 7) 4
    Chapter One 5
    Chapter Two 22
    Chapter Three 43
    Chapter Four 62
    Chapter Five 84
    Chapter Six 98
Cyrus (Iron Tzars MC 8) 113
    Chapter One 114
    Chapter Two 130
    Chapter Three 140
    Chapter Four 148
    Chapter Five 164
    Chapter Six 178
    Chapter Seven 189
    Chapter Eight 205
    Chapter Nine 217
Marteeka Karland 231
Bones MC Multiverse 232
Changeling Press E-Books 233

Eagle (Iron Tzars MC 7)
A Bones MC Romance
Marteeka Karland

Nyla -- Held captive by a monster, I've been forced to service my owner's colleagues while I spied for him. Being really good at my job got me some perks, and Milo treated me better than some -- until the day he caught me in the wrong place at the wrong time. Then my nightmares really began. First chance I get, I run. Straight into the big biker they call Eagle. I don't want to, but I'm falling hard. He swears he'll protect me with his life, and that's just what I'm afraid of. No one runs from Milo... and lives to tell about it.

Eagle -- I have issues. The kind that make me a good person to avoid. Even the club whores stay away from me. My brothers keep a close eye on me, and they shield innocent people from me as much as they can -- until a slip of a woman comes crashing into my life. Beaten and broken, scared out of her mind, she calls to me, soothes the savage beast. She makes me want to believe in love. But when Milo comes after Nyla and threatens my club, I know I'll do whatever it takes to protect her. And I'll claim her, even if she can never accept my darker side.

Chapter One
Eagle

Guard duty. Fuck. When there was a raging party going on with naked club whores all over the Goddamned place. Normally, I'd pass, but I just came back from helping a service buddy clean up a sex trafficking warehouse, and I needed to get the filthy taste outta my mouth. We fucked our girls hard, but they were all ready and willing. They *chose* to be here and always had the power to say no. Guard duty was the very last thing I wanted to be doing.

"Don't even think about wandering off, Eagle. You're stuck here for a reason." Blaze pushed off from where he leaned against the gate. We'd grown up together and the man could almost read my mind at times. He also knew I had a temper on me.

"Never said I was gonna," I grumbled, knowing that was exactly what I intended on doing the first chance I got.

"Yep. I'm here with you because everyone knows you were on edge when you came back from Grim Road's little foray. Everyone knows how you are after a situation like that. You need to let off steam before you're fit for decent company."

"This is not lettin' off steam, you motherfucker." My growl had no heat in it. Mainly because I knew he was right.

"Nope. Since Walker wasn't available to take you huntin' for a couple weeks, it's become my job to find another way for you to loosen up."

I scowled at Blaze. "I don't need no Goddamned babysitter!"

"No. You need a couple weeks in the woods. Or a night or two in the fights. Otherwise, you end up gettin' too rough with the girls, and they're used to rough. As much as they usually love your brand of fuckin', I guaran-damn-tee you ain't a one of 'em willin' to take you on tonight."

I got it. I could be a handful when I was this wound up. "Still don't need no fuckin' babysitter."

"Ain't babysittin' ya. Just watchin' out for my brother." Blaze gripped my shoulder once before lighting his pipe. Man smoked homegrown tobacco. Smelled good but was strong as shit. The scent was soothing, though. Still not as good as beating the shit outta someone. Or hunting in the woods. I'd go to the woods by myself but the last time I did I was gone over a month. When Walker finally found me, I was damned near a wild man. Lost in my own mind, the violence in my past completely overtaking me. It was why I didn't normally go on runs like the one I had with Grim Road. Only reason I had gone on this job was that I owed Rocket a whole hell of a lot from our time in the service.

I was about to walk around the front part of the compound when I heard a strangled sob and the soft patting of bare feet on pavement. Female? Whoever it was, she was running like the hounds of hell were after her.

"Get back here, bitch!"

Blaze and I glanced at each other, both of us moving to the gate entrance. I could see a small figure now. The moon was bright. The second that figure cleared the cover of the trees lining the narrow road, I realized not only was the figure indeed a woman, but she was naked. And terrified.

"Help!" she sobbed and gasped as she approached us. Just as she neared the gate, she stumbled. I lunged for her, catching her slight form in my arms. "Please," she panted, her breath coming in ragged gasps. "Oh, God! Please help me!"

"Where'd she go?"

"Ain't nothin' out here but that MC. They won't let her in. They don't let nobody in."

Two men emerged from the shadows, following the same path the woman had come from. They trotted more sedately. Like they expected she'd stop here and that we'd refuse her entry but might keep her talking long enough for them to catch her.

"Girl," I murmured, looking down into her upturned, terrified face. "They comin' for you?"

She nodded, either unable to or afraid to speak. In my arms, she trembled uncontrollably. The summer air was warm and humid so even though she was naked I didn't think she was cold.

Her hair was a tangled mess, and dirt streaked her face. A long scratch marred one cheek and I thought I saw a bruise darkening the other side of her face. Though she had lush curves, she was short and light in my arms. I thought her hair was either dark blonde or light brown, but it was so matted and dirty it was hard to tell. Even though she didn't wince where my arms were around her, I'd bet my last dollar she was covered in even more bruises.

"You want to go with them?" This from Blaze. I shot him an irritated look, tightening my arms around her. I wasn't protective over women, but something primitive and frightening rose up inside me. There was no way I was letting this woman get hurt on my watch.

"I think it's pretty fuckin' obvious she don't, Blaze."

The other man raised an eyebrow but said nothing else. A few seconds later, the two men chasing her slowed to a walk. One of them raised a hand in greeting.

"Hey there! Thanks for catchin' her."

Neither me nor Blaze said anything. Blaze stepped slightly in front of me and the young woman while I pulled off my cut and shirt, then shoved the tee over her head before urging her to sit just inside the gate in the grass next to the fence. Wasn't much, but hopefully it made her a little more comfortable.

"Wait here," I said softly. She looked at the men with sheer terror and whimpered. "Nope." I pressed my hand to her face and turned her to look at me. "You focus on me." Again, she let out a little whimper before meeting my gaze. "Now. Wait here. We'll get rid of this riffraff, then figure out what's next."

"They'll kill me if you give me back to them." Her voice was barely above a whisper, and she tried to shift her gaze back to the men. Blaze was currently backing them out of the driveway.

"No one said you had to go with them." I kept my tone gentle. She was heartbreakingly lovely, even dirty and terrified as she was. The longer I was in her presence, the more I wanted to wrap her up in a layer of protection and keep her safe from the whole fucking world. And that wasn't me. "Just stay here. We'll take care of this."

She stared at me with the most unusual coppery eyes I'd ever seen. They shone through her tears like new pennies in the silvery moonlight. Then she nodded ever so slightly, and I helped her sit back in the grass before joining Blaze.

"Of course, she wants to come with us," one of the guys was telling Blaze. "She only ran because she thinks she'll make more money with you guys. Little whore's only out for one thing. Right, Mick?"

"Hell, just ten minutes ago she was beggin' me to

come down her throat." Both men laughed.

Blaze glanced at me when I stopped beside him. I shook my head.

"She doesn't want to go with them." I said softly.

"Sorry, guys. Lady doesn't want to leave with you." Blaze's smile wasn't congenial. He looked more like he was looking forward to them trying to force the issue.

"Now wait just a Goddamned minute!" This time, Mick answered. "She's our property. Bought and paid for."

"That so?" Blaze glanced at me before growling at the man. "Who the fuck sold her to you?"

"Mr. Noyb." The other guy said with a smirk. "None Of Your Business."

"Joke's on you, pal. 'Cause I'm makin' it my business." Blaze's hand shot out, snagging him by the throat and squeezed.

"What the fuck?" Mick stumbled backward. I lunged for the smaller man and held him in a similar hold with my fist around his neck.

"Who sold you that girl?" Blaze repeated. "Name. Contact info. Or I strangle the fuckin' life outta you."

"We stole her off the streets, man!" Mick said, his eyes bulging. His hand clawed at mine, but I just squeezed harder. "Watched her daddy leave while she was in a gas station restroom! I swear!"

Blaze took his radio off his belt. "Brick. Roman. Gonna need the barn. Got two pissants at the gate who need a little education."

There was a silence before I heard Brick's voice over the radio. "Copy. Be at the gate in five."

"She ain't no toddler," I snapped. "You didn't just take her from her daddy. How'd you get your fuckin' hands on her?"

"Dude, shut up!" Mick hissed at his companion.

"I ain't dyin' for that bastard. It was all great when he promised no one would miss her. He might not turn her in missin', but these guys sure the fuck will."

"He's wrong, you know," I commented. "We ain't filin' a missin' person's report. You're gonna die because of what you've already done."

The guy's bladder let go and he whimpered. "Please, mister! It wasn't my idea!"

"Shut! Up! They're gonna kill us no matter what we do, Caleb!"

"Yep." Blaze grinned at Mick, tilting his head sideways and getting right in the guy's face. His voice was soft and menacing. Hell, if he'd been in my face looking like he was at this guy, I'd have paused to reflect on my own misdeeds. "Only question is how hard you die. It can be a quick, easy bullet to the head, or you can last a few weeks. Choice is yours. But don't think that few weeks will be spent in comfort." The smile Blaze's lips widened into wasn't pleasant.

"Look," Caleb said, frantically looking from me to Blaze and back. "The guy said he was her daddy. Gave us five thousand dollars to kidnap her and keep her quiet for a couple of weeks. Said if he needed us to look after her longer than that, he'd double it."

"He tell you to hurt her?"

Caleb's lips tried to turn up into a smile, but he was too scared to pull it off. "Just said to convince her to keep her mouth shut or she'd get more of whatever we did to her. Said as long as she was alive, he didn't care."

I glanced at Blaze. His expression was hard. Angry. "Right."

"We wasn't gonna hurt her, man!"

"Uh-huh. That's why she's runnin' as hard as she could go, barefoot and naked, begging two fuckin' scary, big-ass bikers like us to help her." Blaze snorted. "You believe that shit, right Eagle?"

"Sure. Happens to me all the fuckin' time." I glanced at the girl. She was huddled as small as she could get, her knees under the T-shirt and her arms clasped around them. "She's scratched up and has a bruise on the side of her face." I looked back at the guys. "She gonna have bruises anywhere else on her body?"

"How'm I s'posed t' know!" Mick yelled at me, struggling against Blaze now. "She probably got a bunch of bruises before we got her. We never done nuttin' to her."

The girl still stared wide-eyed at us, not moving a muscle other than to breathe. Didn't take a rocket scientist to know she was terrified.

"Right." Blaze brought his fist back, then connected with Mick's nose. Blood splattered out both sides of his fist and the guy screamed.

"What's the matter, Mick?" Blaze asked, getting right up in the guy's face. He still held Mick by the throat. "Can dish it out but can't take it?"

"I didn't do anything!" he screamed.

I looked back at the girl still huddling in the grass by the chain link fence. "He hit your face, darlin'?" Her eyes got wide, and she looked back and forth between Mick and Caleb, obviously not sure what to say. "Look at me." My voice was hard, brooking no argument. She obeyed the instant the words were out of my mouth, but her gaze immediately went back to the two men she'd been running from. "Nope. Eyes on me, honey."

Surprisingly, she obeyed. "That's good. Keep your eyes on me. You good?"

She didn't move for several seconds, then she nodded her head almost imperceptibly.

"Good. Now, tell me. Did they hit your face? Put that bruise and scratch there?"

One tear streaked from her eye down her cheek. She ignored it but nodded her head again. Stronger this time.

"What happened?" Brick approached the gate with Atlas in tow.

I shoved Caleb away from me, scowling at him. He knew better than to try and take off. Kid was starting to cry now. The other one looked disgruntled but wasn't fighting. For now. Personally, I was hoping that'd change.

I pointed to the girl. "She was runnin' from these two twits. Says they're the ones who hit her."

Brick glanced at the girl, then back at the twits in question. "What's their story?"

"Claim the girl's dad paid them to hold onto her a while. Instructions were not to kill her, and to convince her to keep her mouth shut about something. Ain't sure if it was this incident or somethin' else." I was so angry I was barely holding on to my control. The only thing that kept me from unleashing hell on these two punks was the girl huddled by the fence. I was afraid more violence would break her.

"Yeah, but I think they'd've done it just for the thrill of it." Blaze shook his head. "They ain't exactly what I'd call wholesome young men."

"They got more women other than you, girl?" Brick's voice was gruff and angry. It was easy to see he was out for blood with this. Iron Tzars tried to keep a low profile, but we also protected the people in our territory as best we could. Which meant predators in the community didn't live long, their bodies never found.

Again, she shifted her gaze to the two men who'd been chasing her. When she looked back at me this time, her gaze clung to mine. "Yes," she breathed out. "There were two others. Mistakes."

"Were?" Atlas barked out the question and she flinched, shrinking in on herself before nodding. "They get away?"

"No." She touched her lips with her fingertips, like she was trying to keep her mouth shut but seemed helpless to not answer our questions. "They..." She swallowed, shaking her head slightly, a sob escaping her. "They're dead."

"Mistakes?" Brick was trying to rein it in, but he was as furious as the rest of us. His barked question not only made the girl flinch but shrink in on herself.

"Hey," I said, softening my tone. "Remember? Eyes on me." I approached her and crouched down so I wasn't towering over her. "What do you mean 'mistakes,' Brick?"

"Did they kill the women accidentally or did they mean to kill them?"

She shook her head. "Deliberate."

"Fuck." Brick scrubbed a hand over his face. "We ain't had this kinda trouble in Evansville in a long fuckin' time. Come on," he said, motioning for the men to move in front of him. "Zip-tie their hands, then get 'em to the barn. Put 'em with the other two. Maybe if they see what they're in for we can get some more answers from them."

"She's lying!" Mick screamed. He was still defiant, but there was real fear in his eyes now. "She's just tryin' to get us in trouble!"

Brick snorted. "In trouble?" He shook his head, chuckling lightly as he glanced at Atlas. "Is this guy for real?"

Atlas shook his head sadly. "Son, this ain't high school. You don't 'get in trouble.' You are way the fuck past 'in trouble'."

"Where did these fucks come from? They can't have been far. She was running too hard. And naked." Brick pulled his phone from his pocket, pressed something on the screen, then held the phone to his ear. "Wylde. Got a couple dumb shits I need a hit on. Yeah, I'll get you pics. Hang on." Brick snapped an image of each man and sent them to Wylde, our tech guy. For good measure, he searched them, coming out with their wallets. He took their licenses and sent those images to Wylde as well, then put the phone back to his ear. "Got it? Good. We're headed to the barn. Meet us there when you have something. Need to know where they live or where they might have come from in this area." When he disconnected, Brick jerked his head to indicate deeper into the compound. "Let's go. We'll take these guys out as soon as Clutch has a cage ready."

"What about the girl?" I'd tried to keep my mind focused on the men, but it wasn't them I was interested in. There was something about the woman that caught my attention and refused to let me go.

"Take her to Stitches," Brick ordered. "He can assess her injuries and tell us where we need to go from there. I'll get Sting to send the old ladies to the clinic. That way she won't feel so outnumbered."

I nodded, but didn't much care if the women were there or not. I'd be there. "Come on, honey. Let's get you inside where you can clean up. Doc's gonna take a look at you. Help you with anything that might need doctorin' or some shit." Yeah. I wasn't good with words.

"You sound like a moron," Blaze chuckled. "Doctorin'? Who the fuck says that?"

"Shut up, you piece of shit." I wasn't mad at Blaze. It's how we worked. He knew that and clapped me on the back with a soft chuckle.

"I predict someone's givin' up his man card real soon." Blaze poked me as he shoved Dumb and Dumber on ahead of us so they followed Brick and Atlas while Blaze and me would follow behind with Cyrus, who'd stepped out of the shadows to assist. As soon as I got my woman ready to come with me.

"Get on with yourself. Make sure those dumbasses don't try to bolt. I'll be there in a second."

"Take your time, man. Cyrus and me got this. Don't spook her."

"I think she's already spooked." I held out my hand to the girl while I continued to crouch in front of her. "Can you come with me? Ain't gonna hurt you. Nothin' happens you don't want."

"C-can I h-have some w-water?" Her voice was a little rough and a lot wobbly. I had no doubt she was thirsty. Not to mention terrified out of her mind.

"You can have whatever you want, honey. Food. Water. A hot bath. The last one in private. Once Stitches has looked you over, I'll find a place where you can rest safely. Sleep as long as you like. Rest. Heal."

She shook her head. "Just some w-water."

"How about we talk about it later? I'll take you inside, and we'll get you that water. Then we'll go from there. Can you do that for me?"

She looked at me for a long time. I wasn't sure she was going to answer me but she finally nodded her head. "O-OK." Gingerly, she took my hand and I stood slowly, helping her to her feet.

"Can't walk on this gravel in bare feet. Can I pick you up? Carry you to the clubhouse?"

With a curious tilt of her head, she looked like she might ask a question. Instead, she just nodded. I didn't wait for anything more. I scooped her up and followed the others toward the main clubhouse on the compound grounds. The brothers were waiting on Clutch when I reached them, the girl securely in my arms. It really should have been more difficult than it was, but not only was I fucking strong, the woman was light as a feather.

"You need anything from her?" I asked Brick as I climbed the stairs leading to the porch.

"I think I got it all from Blaze. If I have questions, I'll come find her. You stayin' tonight, darlin'?"

I looked down at the woman in my arms. She was stiff, not relaxed at all, but the second she realized Brick wanted her to answer the question, she wrapped her arms around my neck and buried her face in my chest. I'd be lying if my shoulders didn't go back just that little bit. On some mysterious level, she already trusted me. I'd given her no reason to, and I was a fucking surly bastard, but she'd thrown her lot in with me and I knew I'd do anything to keep that trust.

"Guess that's my answer." Brick gave me a hard look. "You be careful with that girl. You ain't fit for company since you came back from Grim Road. It's obvious she's not up to dealing with your normal charming self, let alone the way you get after that kinda violence."

"I hear you, brother. I've got it under control."

"Anytime you think you might need a break to regroup, you call Blaze. You can't get him, call me."

"Swear," I acknowledged. "I'm good."

Brick nodded and I turned to take my charge to Stitches, our club doctor. He must have gotten word from someone we were headed that way because he met us outside the clinic.

"Anything obviously major?" Stitches could be brisk on the best of days, but he was always gentle, especially when he had to treat the women in the compound. As I approached, his gaze was firmly fixed on the woman in my arms. Fuck. I didn't even know her name!

"Bruised all to shit. Scared out of her mind. Ain't sure otherwise."

"Bring her inside."

She continued to tremble and made one small whimper as I climbed the steps to the clinic Stitches had set up for the club. Once inside, I set her on the stretcher and stepped away. Again, she pulled the shirt I'd given her over her knees, wrapping her arms around herself protectively. Her eyes were wide and wild as she took stock of her surroundings. I got a water bottle from the fridge before approaching her again.

"What's your name, girl?"

"N-Nyla." Her voice was almost a whisper, and her gaze zeroed in on the bottle I held. I handed it to her without opening it. She took it gingerly with shaking hands. When she struggled to untwist the lid, she trembled even more, a frustrated, desperate sound escaping her.

"Want me to help?" I didn't want to push her. "Was afraid you wouldn't like the seal being broken before I handed it to you."

She nodded but didn't say anything. She also didn't hand the bottle back to me but continued to struggle on her own. When it became obvious that, one, she couldn't open it herself and, two, she really wanted the contents, I stepped over to her and placed my hand on her shoulder. Without a word, I covered her hand holding the bottle with my own to brace it while I opened the lid with my other hand. Once I let her go, she gripped the bottle in both her tiny hands and *guzzled* the contents.

"Hey, there," I said, moving the bottle away from her lips gently. "Don't make yourself sick." She looked up at me, and I thought she might growl like a feral kitten. If the situation hadn't been what it was, I might have grinned at her, but I knew she likely hadn't had anything to drink in a while.

"What's going on?" Stitches frowned at me as he entered the room with a blanket and some sweats and a T-shirt. He laid them on the stretcher beside her.

"Just trying to keep her from pukin'. She's thirsty."

Stitches grunted but didn't say anything else. Instead, he took his stethoscope from around his neck and put it in his ears. "Just gonna listen to your lungs and heart. You OK with that?"

Nyla nodded her head but didn't move. Stitches was patient with her, starting with her back as he listened carefully. Then her sides.

There was a knock at the door.

"Come in."

Atlas's woman stepped inside the room and gave Nyla a soft smile. "I'm Rose. Are you with Eagle?" Rose was at least five months pregnant and sporting a rounded tummy. She caressed her baby bump absently as she spoke to Nyla.

Nyla shook her head, but her gaze darted in my direction briefly. I wasn't sure what I saw on her face, but it almost looked like a plea. For me to leave her alone? Or for me to claim her? Would make sense she'd want me to leave her alone. She'd likely want to stay as far from strange men as she could. But something inside my gut told me that wasn't the case. Nyla wanted me to stake a claim on her. Not to make her mine, but to give her my protection. Now, that I could believe.

"Yeah. She's with me. You make sure everyone knows. Yeah?"

Rose smiled knowingly. "Somehow, I don't think that will be a problem. It's pretty easy to see."

I frowned at the woman, but she just smiled as she stepped farther into the room. "I'm going to help Stitches, Nyla." She spoke deliberately to Nyla, and I was suddenly grateful to my brothers for sending Rose. She would help Nyla to know she wasn't surrounded and that someone was watching out for her. "We're not going to expose you. We're not going to touch you in any way you don't consent to, and never for anything other than clinical reasons."

Stitches stood in the background watching Nyla without being too threatening. Abrasive or not, I couldn't deny the man could read his patients correctly. There was no way Nyla could tolerate either of us in close proximity for long. Rose, with her sweet and gentle personality, would put her more at ease.

No one rushed her or tried more to coerce her. Rose's smile was understanding and patient. Like she could wait all day for whatever answer Nyla gave. I was about to call a halt, to tell them all we'd wait until Nyla had rested when she turned her gaze to me. For a woman so vulnerable, she was fucking hard to read. More than anything I wanted her to be comfortable. I didn't want her to feel like we were violating her all over again, but I needed to make sure she didn't have an injury that needed immediate treatment.

"I promise I won't let anyone hurt you, Nyla." I tried to sound soothing when I was feeling anxious. My chest was tight with worry, and I wanted to will her to let Stitches check her over. "I'll be right here."

Finally, she nodded her head and slid her legs down the stretcher out in front of her, dropping her arms beside her. Her lower lip trembled ever so slightly before she tugged it inside her mouth with her teeth.

For several minutes Rose and Stitches fussed over Nyla. Rose washed any scrapes and cuts she had while Stitches gave instructions. The only time he invaded Nyla's personal space was to listen to her heart and look into her eyes and ears. The rest of the time he let Rose be the one to take care of her.

"Fortunately, it doesn't look like you're physically harmed." Nyla had denied the men had raped her, though she'd indicated they'd tried. Stitches crossed his arms over his chest as he spoke. He looked at me, but he was talking to Nyla. "You're dehydrated and hungry, but otherwise there's no lasting physical injuries. The mental trauma, however, is something altogether different. I don't normally like to prescribe sleeping pills, but you may need something. I'll also give you something for pain tonight so you can rest easier."

Rose handed her a backpack. "There's some essentials in there. Bathroom stuff, hairbrush, toothbrush, a couple changes of clothing. Underwear and socks still in the pack. If you need other things, just let me know." Rose nodded at me. "Eagle can get a hold of Atlas. He's my husband. I'll make sure to get you mine and the other old ladies' phone numbers tomorrow."

"Thank you." Nyla's voice was so soft I had to strain to hear. Rose smiled at her, squeezing her hand gently.

"Trust in Eagle. If he says you're his, he'll protect you with his last breath. All the men here are like that."

Something inside me shifted. For weeks, I'd been immersed in the worst society had to offer. The sex ring I'd helped Grim Road take down made me want to kill and puke all at the same time. I left that job so very angry, needing to kill when that hadn't been my job. I was the spotter. The tracker. I'd brought the men of Grim Road to their door only to back into the shadows and wait for instructions. Mostly, they kept me out of the action because I couldn't handle violence and keep my sanity. Once I started fighting, I didn't stop until I killed someone. Or everyone in the immediate vicinity. It was a fight or flight reflex I'd had since childhood, growing up on the streets. Fighting had always been life or death. And I loved living.

Now, all that anger and aggression was transformed into a protective force I wasn't sure I was ready for. Every ounce of it focused on one small woman sitting beside me looking lost, hurt, and terrified.

No. Not on my watch. Challenge issued. Challenge accepted.

Chapter Two
Nyla

I didn't know what to do. Didn't know who to trust or what my next move was. Did I even have a move? I might have jumped from the frying pan into the fire. I had no idea where I'd been running to. My only thought was to find someone to help me. To get me away and someplace safe. I'd heard Mick and Caleb say this place was an MC. I assumed they meant motorcycle club, and figured I might as well figure out a way to kill myself right then because the rest of my life promised to be worse than death. Then I'd stumbled into the arms of Eagle. I didn't exactly trust him and could almost feel the violence radiating from him. He wasn't a safe man, to be sure.

Then he had to go and defend me against my nightmares. I'd been captive for a month and those two assholes were growing braver and braver, getting closer and closer to raping me. I was certain it would have happened tonight if I hadn't managed to get away.

Now I was in some kind of compound, surrounded by a chain-link fence topped with razor wire. If it weren't for Eagle, I might have been even more terrified. The gentle way he was with me was at odds with the anger I felt in the hard lines of his chest and arms. I had the feeling it had very little to do with me and more like it was simmering just beneath the surface.

"I can set you up with your own room if you like," Rose offered. "You'll have all the privacy you need and be completely safe to rest and heal."

"Thanks," I whispered. "I'd just like something to drink. Maybe something to eat. Just that and I'll go."

"Like hell." Eagle lay a hand on my shoulder, squeezing lightly. It was something between encouragement and a warning. I wasn't sure which, but he didn't hurt me.

"You don't have to stay with Eagle if you don't want to," Rose said quickly. "I think he's wanting to take you with him, but that's your decision. I can vouch for him if it will make you feel better. My husband trusts him implicitly. Eagle is very loyal and dedicated. He'll be a good protector for you."

God, I wanted to stay! I was probably stupid, but this place felt safer than I'd ever felt in my life. Even before I was given to Milo. It was all in how they'd treated me since I ran into Eagle's arms. Literally. No one had commented on my lack of clothing other than to assume I was in trouble. They'd been unfailingly careful with me. Eagle had held my naked form in his arms as intimately as a man could hold a woman and hadn't reacted with anything other than compassion and urgency to get me help. They'd shown me more respect in the past half hour than I'd had from anyone my entire life.

"I w-want to s-stay," I stuttered out. I think I was in some kind of shock or something. The adrenaline leached out of my body with each passing second, making me shake in withdrawal. "But I d-don't know..."

"I'll treat you good, honey." Eagle place a finger on my jaw to gently turn my face up to his. "No one will get to you unless you want them in. That includes me. You want me outside the door keepin' guard, that's what I'll do."

That surprised me and I gasped in a breath. "I can't ask you t-to do th-that."

"Your call."

I thought a moment. My mind was whirling in a million different directions and my heart started to pound. "I'm not s-sure any decision I make n-now would b-be the right o-one."

"Nyla." Stitches snapped in a crisp voice, surprising me. I'd forgotten he was still in the room. I jumped and moved closer to Eagle before I'd even realized it. Stitches raised an eyebrow at Eagle. "I think that settles that. You might not realize you trust him, Nyla, but buried in there, your instincts trust him. I'll let Brick and Sting know you're under his protection, but they will want to confirm that with you. If you change your mind, all you have to do is say so."

"OK. I guess I'll just go with my gut, then." I looked up at Eagle. "I don't know why you're helping me, but I'm grateful. I probably latched on to you because it was you who kept me from falling when I stumbled."

"Whatever makes you comfortable. Until we can get this sorted out and help you get back where you belong, we'll make sure you're as comfortable as you can be."

"Where I belong…" I hadn't realized I'd spoken out loud until Rose gave me a strange look. Like she was trying to understand what I meant. "I don't belong anywhere." I tried to smile, but it was a pitiful attempt at best.

Before Rose could question me, Eagle tossed a blanket around my shoulders and scooped me up in his arms. The backpack Rose had given me fell to the floor when I started. I was still dressed in his T-shirt, but the ends of the blanket covered my thighs and draped over my side. Hopefully it covered my ass if my shirt tail wasn't caught by his arm under my legs. Of all the things to worry about, I was horrified at the thought of someone seeing my bare ass. If that was the worst thing that happened to me here, I'd count it a fucking win.

I didn't consider myself overweight, but I wasn't skinny either. I carried some weight on my hips, ass, and boobs. At least, I had before I'd been brought to this place. To the two men who'd been tormenting me for the last few weeks. This guy carried me as easily as he might have a child, taking stairs two at a time and moving deeper into the building. Rose followed us, though she had to trot to keep up. She kept pace with Eagle's long strides.

When he got to the room he wanted, he set me between him and the door, keeping his back to Rose and the huge man who was coming up behind Rose. The door opened and he carried me inside. He tried to kick the door shut, but the other man caught it with the slap of his palm.

"Atlas, now ain't the time," Eagle growled at the man entering the room behind him.

"Rose has your woman's shit. And I know you ain't being a bastard to my pregnant wife."

Rose covered her grin with a hand as she looked up and met my gaze. There was a pull to Rose as someone I wanted to befriend, same as there was with wanting Eagle for protection. But I had no idea what to think or do with anything else. I wasn't even really sure about Eagle. He was the one who'd pulled me out of my nightmare. I would probably have latched on to any of them if they'd gotten to me first. Maybe.

I liked this guy. He was gentle with me even if he was a bit gruff. He handled me like he thought I might shatter and to be honest, I thought I might. It felt like he was the glue holding me together. They'd taken care of Mick and Caleb and none of the men or women here had hurt me. In fact, they were taking care of me. How long that lasted was anyone's guess.

Eagle snarled over his shoulder as he moved to the back of the room to a shut door. "Fine. Give us a minute." He set me down and opened the door to a surprisingly clean and neat bathroom.

"I'll be back with some clothes for you." Eagle grasped my chin in his hand. "You're safe here, girl. We're all gonna protect you."

Though I wasn't completely convinced, I nodded my head anyway. I'd put my trust here for now, with these people. Well, mostly with Eagle. I knew absolutely nothing about them other than they hadn't turned me away and had seemed angry that I'd been hurt. So far, they'd checked my wounds and dressed them, given me water, and offered me a place to stay with someone I was comfortable with. Maybe it made me impossibly naive, but I thought it was best to take it day by day. Maybe even hour by hour. At the first sign of trouble, I'd bail. Assuming I could get away.

Eagle shut the door behind him only to return soon after, knocking and waiting for me to open the door myself and not bursting in on me. When I did, he grunted his approval and handed me a backpack.

"Got shit in there. Rose said you dropped it when I picked you up." He shifted from one foot to the other and refused to meet my gaze. Almost like he was uncomfortable about something, though I had no idea what it could be. "The girls put it together with what they had so if the sizes ain't right we'll fix it tomorrow. Ain't got a bathtub, but you're welcome to the shower if you want. I can have Stitches redress everything if you do."

I nodded. "Thank you."

"Towels under the sink. Should be a toothbrush

in the medicine cabinet I haven't opened yet. Clean up, then come to the couch. Sting and Iris'll want to talk to you. Make sure you're good with this arrangement."

Again, I nodded. I knew I needed to say something else but couldn't form words or thoughts. I was crashing. Hard. It was going to be hard to function soon, as the panic faded and my body shut down. Even still, I wanted a shower in the worst way, but didn't think it was the wisest idea. The last place I needed to let my guard down was in a strange man's territory where all his friends had his back.

God! I didn't know what to do! I was still standing there when there was another knock at the door.

"Nyla? You good?" His voice was like silk over gravel. If I let myself get lost in the sound, he'd have me prisoner just the same as Mick and Caleb. And Milo. I shivered just thinking the name and quickly shut that part of my brain down. I couldn't think about that right now. If I did, I'd lose what little hold I had left on my sanity.

"Yep."

"Open up. You dressed?"

I froze, not knowing how to answer. If I said, yes, he'd probably open the door, but if I said no, I'd have to explain why I hadn't showered yet. Last thing I wanted to do was insult the people who'd saved me.

"Nyla?"

I opened the door a crack and looked up into Eagle's dark, dark eyes. He glanced down at my form at what he could see through the small opening and frowned.

"You didn't want a shower?"

"I-I wasn't s-sure..."

"If you don't want to get in the shower, you can

use the washcloths next to the towels. Just do what you're comfortable with. The cleaner you are, the better you'll feel."

I tore my gaze away from Eagle's, fixing on a point on the floor. I knew I needed to bathe, but if I got naked I'd be even more vulnerable. Then again, maybe I was overthinking the whole thing. God! I was so confused and scared!

"Go on. Clean up so you can sleep easier later. Ain't nobody gonna be in here until you're ready. Get me?"

I nodded, not sure if I got him or not. I hated feeling like this! I wasn't generally an indecisive person. I had to make decisions frequently to get whatever information Milo had tasked me with. But my mind wasn't working the way it should right now. The shock of what had happened to me, the knowledge that I had information Milo didn't want me to have and had obviously considered shutting me up permanently, was a huge blow for me. I knew I wasn't always safe with Milo and his men, but I knew what to expect and how to avoid everyone's wrath. By running, I'd gone against everything I'd learned about how to survive.

When he didn't shut the door, I looked up at him again. "Go on," he encouraged. "You can do this. Shower. Dress. Out of the bathroom. Once you open the door, I'll take over."

That sounded better. Had poor decisions not led me to this situation, I'd probably have resented him telling me he'd take over. Right now, though, I couldn't figure out what decision to make. Run or trust the man who'd saved me.

I could do this.

Stitches had cleaned and dressed several shallow

cuts and scrapes to my knees. The side of my face felt swollen and hot. My cheek throbbed and my head was starting to hurt. And yeah. I felt grubby as hell.

I took my time, trying to use the heated water and the gentle way the spray worked my muscles to comfort myself and relax a little. I didn't wash, exactly. More like I let the water pour over me. My hair was damp, but I hadn't stuck my head under the spray yet. I was still numb, not sure what to do or expect. I couldn't even contemplate that I may well have landed in a worse situation that I was in before. If these guys were toying with me, playing me for some sadistic reason, they were doing a damned good job of it.

There was another light knock at the door. I'd just turned off the water and had reached for a towel to dry off, but I froze.

"You good, Nyla?" Eagle again. Was he hanging out just outside the door? Why? My heart started pounding and I shivered again. I tried to hurry and get my clothes on, but I was shaking so hard I could barely stay upright. "Nyla? Honey, talk to me."

My breath was coming in wheezing gasps as panic blanketed me. Somehow, I managed to get the panties in the plastic packaging open and one leg through the opening of a pair, but I was still mostly wet and I fumbled with the other leg.

The door cracked open. "Nyla?"

The second Eagle stuck his head through the opening, something inside me snapped. I screamed, throwing something at the door. I had no idea what it was. I just picked up the first thing my hand touched and threw it to defend myself.

"Hey. Easy, Nyla. No one's gonna hurt you." The reply was calm, but Eagle didn't open the door again. "Do you want me to get Rose?"

I couldn't speak, my breath sawing in and out of my lungs in huge gasps. Couldn't do anything but struggle to breathe. Trembling and shaking, I sat on the closed toilet lid, my knees tucked to my chest. I still had my underwear around one ankle and the towel around my shoulders. Voices could be heard outside the door, but Eagle didn't open it again. Maybe he'd go away. Did I want him to go away?

The next thing I knew, Rose entered the bathroom and shut the door softly. "Hey there." She smiled at me but didn't get closer. "Can I help you dress? You won't feel as vulnerable if you're dressed."

Meeting her gaze was hard. I felt like an idiot, but I couldn't seem to bring myself out of the panic engulfing me. "I'm s-so s-sor-ry," I sobbed out. "S-sorry!"

"Nothing to be sorry about," Rose said with a kind smile. "You've been through enough to make anyone have issues. You're here in a strange place with strange people. Of course, you're scared." Rose picked up the backpack and pulled out some more clothes. She put a T-shirt over my head before helping me with my underwear and a pair of thin cotton pants. Something loose and easy to move around in, as well as cool in the hot, summer weather. Right now, I seemed to be equal parts hot and cold. I was sweating, but I couldn't seem to stop shaking.

"W-what's gonna h-happen to m-me?" I hated that I couldn't control myself but everything was hitting me all at once now that my escape had been successful and the immediate danger had passed.

Rose's expression was startled. "Nothing bad. I promise. Is there someone you need me to call for you? You're not a prisoner, Nyla. No one's going to hurt you. There're more old ladies here ready to help you besides me. I was just the one in the compound when the guys found you. If you don't believe me, you need to talk to Serelda and Winter. They've both been through some pretty bad times before they came here. It was a long time ago and they lived in another MC that protected them after their trauma, but if they feel safe here, there's nothing for you to fear."

"The men… Will they give me back to those two guys? Or take me back to the man who gave me to them?"

"They said it was your father. Is that not accurate?" Rose's questions were asked gently as she finished helping me dress.

"No. I don't have a family." It was the truth. I'd been on my own since thirteen. My mom died when I was born, and my dad had been strung out most of the time. I'd been passed around from place to place by people who'd hurt me over and over. Men. Women. Whoever had been willing to pay. Until Milo had taken me in. It had been better, but he was still selling me. The difference was I'd been given to older, wealthy, powerful men who treated me as less than they were, but had no interest in really hurting me. Just fucking me. Or watching me fuck someone else. "It's my experience that people don't help you unless they want something in return. I'm not fucking anyone here. I'm done with that no matter what happens. I'd rather die than let myself be sold again. I hated every second of it!" The more I said out loud, the more anxious I became. I meant what I said, but I was also terrified I couldn't stick to my guns.

"No one expects you to, honey." She met my gaze with her own. The woman was lovely and gentle, but I could see there was a core of steel running through her. I could tell by the hard look in her eyes she meant what she said. "Sex should be something beautiful and fun. Not something you only do in payment for something, unless you enjoy that sort of thing. It's certainly not something someone should take from you."

"I'll fight anyone who tries." I needed her to understand me. To know that they might be able to force me, but I'd wouldn't go down willingly. "They all might be bigger and stronger than me, but I'll never give up."

"Anyone here tries to force you, you come to me. Or any of the old ladies. We will shut that shit down and kill a motherfucker trying to hurt you like that. If you believe nothing else, believe that."

"They're all stronger than you, too." I felt helpless, but for the first time in my life, I thought I felt a spark of hope that she might be telling the truth. She could be deceiving me. Lord knew I'd been lied to before, but it didn't feel like deception. "How could you help me? I'm sure you have your own battles to fight."

"Our men are good men. All the men of Iron Tzars are. There's a few they've weeded out over the last few months, but even the men they removed weren't evil. Not to women and children." She tilted her head to the side before speaking again, like she was trying to figure out the best way to phrase her next words. "We live by our own code here, Nyla. I'm not saying everyone is a law-abiding citizen, but there are lines we don't cross. We protect our territory and the people in it."

I nodded my head when I didn't really understand at all, but honestly, I wasn't certain I wanted to understand what she meant. I just wanted to feel safe. To not be afraid someone was going to jump me if I dozed off. I'd lived like that all my life. Sleep wasn't something I'd ever welcomed.

"Come on. The others should be here now. We'll make sure you have everything you need before we leave you to rest."

Again, I nodded and followed her out of the bathroom like I was in a daze. The second I emerged I took stock of my surroundings. There were more men and women in the small suite now, all talking in quiet murmurs. They didn't stop when I entered the room, rather, Eagle held out an arm to me like he fully expected me to go to him. The funny thing was, before I realized what I was doing, I had moved to his side. Eagle wrapped that arm around my shoulders before leaning in to speak softly into my ear.

"You good?"

"I'm sorry I freaked out. I shouldn't have thrown something at you. I don't even know what it was."

"Surprised you didn't freak out before then. We're not exactly what I'd call a restful bunch. It seems like you've been through the wringer. Just know you're safe here. We'll all protect you. And just between you and me?" He grinned at me. "I'd have thrown something at me long before you did. Don't worry about any of it. You're safe. I swear it."

"Thank you. For this and for before." I wanted to look up into his face but couldn't bear to see pity shining there. Because, honestly, how could these men and women who were so strong and put together not pity someone like me? And they didn't know the full story.

"You're welcome." He urged me to the couch. "Sit."

Even though I was uncomfortable with so many strangers I owed them whatever time they wanted from me. They had questions. The least I could do was give them any answers they wanted.

A man sitting across from me spoke matter-of-factly. "I know there's a lot of people here, Nyla. I'm sorry you haven't had time to get to know us before we start throwing questions at you, but we need to understand what we're facing here. I'm Sting, the president of Iron Tzars. You'll meet my wife, Iris, shortly. Brick was at the gate after Eagle and Blaze brought you inside. He's my vice president. You'll also meet his woman and her sister."

"Yes. I remember. Thank you for letting me stay." I tried to look at the big man in question, but couldn't. I knew better. I was never supposed to catch the attention of anyone. The easiest way to do that was to meet their gaze. It was a rule I'd forgotten over the last hour, but I needed to put my guard back up. These people were helping me now, but God only knew how long that arrangement would continue.

"No thanks necessary." Brick sounded kind. Not harsh like he had at the gate. He was quite possibly the biggest man I'd ever seen, yet he managed to blend into the background when he chose. At the gate he was terrifying and very much in charge. Now, he sat very still and spoke softly. I wondered if that was for my benefit or if he was always like this when not in a hostile environment. Even as big and intimidating as he was, Brick knew how to diminish his presence. I'd only seen a couple of men in my life who either had that ability or the patience to develop it. Most simply steamrolled their way through any situation giving them pushback.

"Do you feel up to talking with us?" Sting asked. "I know I'm pushing you by being here now, but the sooner we know what we're facing, the better we'll be able to protect you."

"I'm so sorry," I said. "I didn't want to get anyone else involved, but I didn't really have a plan other than running like hell. If you hadn't been at the gate when I first got there, they'd have dragged me back and probably killed me."

"When did they take you?" Sting was persistent but gentle in his tone of voice. As much as I didn't want to talk about any of this, I owed them an explanation if I expected any help from them. If I'd known how to help myself, I'd have left and gone my own way. I didn't have that ability and I knew it. I'd been cut off from the world my entire life. Sure, a few of the men I'd been given to had allowed me access to television so I wasn't completely ignorant, but never having lived on the outside, I knew just enough to know I had no hope of making it on my own. Not without someone explaining things to me.

"Those two got me about three weeks ago."

There was silence, and I knew Sting expected me to continue but I didn't really know what to tell him.

"So, they've had you for three weeks. They tried to say your father told them to keep you and convince you to keep your mouth shut. That sound right?"

I shrugged.

"Come on, honey." I jumped when Eagle spoke even though his voice wasn't loud. He leaned in and made his words soft and cajoling close to my ear. "No one's gonna hurt you or judge you or not believe you in general. Just tell Sting what happened so he can look into the situation. We don't like to make decisions without verifying all the facts." Eagle sounded like he was choosing his words carefully. Like he was trying to tell me something without actually spelling it out.

"I belong to a man called Milo. He gives me to

people. Sometimes." My voice was barely above a whisper. It was all I could manage. Thinking about what Milo would do to me when he caught me made me want to vomit. No one left Milo. Ever.

Oh, God! What was I doing? Running from Mick and Caleb had been pure instinct on my part. I'd watched them brutally kill the other two women in the house with me. We'd done as we were told and tried to please the men. It wasn't like we'd disobeyed. I'd belonged to Milo since I was a young teen. He'd taken me off the street and offered me a better life. I'd always known I was property to pass around at Milo's whim, but there were rules. I knew that, if I wanted to continue my comfortable life, I had to obey the rules. The most important rule was *never* to run from Milo.

I'd seen what happened to a few of the girls who ran, and it was never pretty. Yet, when Caleb and Mick beaten the other women to death while they'd fucked them, I'd panicked. I was used to violence, but never so close to me and never directed at me. I was obedient and good at pleasing the men or women Milo had given me to because I knew it was what I had to do to repay Milo's kindness in taking me in. I saw to it Milo's friends had a good time and in return Milo let me live in relative luxury.

Until three weeks ago. Until I saw something I shouldn't have.

"I--I can't... breathe..." My breath came in harsh gasps and my stomach heaved. Standing, I turned and sprinted for the bathroom, skidding to a halt on my knees in front of the toilet where I vomited violently. There wasn't really anything in my stomach to lose except the water I'd been given and some foul-smelling bile.

Tears streamed down my face both from fear and

the violence with which I vomited. When I collapsed back on my ass, someone flushed the toilet and handed me a wet washcloth. Another person held my hair back and handed me a glass of water. I rinsed my mouth and spat it out in the toilet before flushing it again.

"I'm dead. Milo would've killed me for running, but running to an MC? He'll make me die hard."

"Nobody's gonna hurt you, girl." I turned my head to find Eagle giving me a steady gaze as he brushed hair off my face. The dark strands were grungy and damp where I hadn't washed it in the shower, but the spray had hit me.

"N-no one l-leaves Milo." My voice came out a strangled whisper. "No one."

"Tell me who Milo is, Nyla." Eagle's voice was soft and coaxing even as it was commanding.

"He's a monster."

"Do you know his full name?"

I shook my head. "Just Milo. But everyone is afraid of him. I'm afraid of him." Eagle clenched his jaw, and I knew he was upset. Probably thought I couldn't give him the information he wanted. "If I knew his name or even any other name he goes by, I'd tell you. He's the last person I want to find me right now, and the last person you want to get mixed up with. I've heard them say everyone watches him because if he's coming for them, they want enough time to kill themselves before he can catch them."

"Who's everyone?" Eagle took the cloth from me and wiped my face gently.

"Everyone I've ever met. Even the guys who are rich and powerful. The men he gave me to for whatever reason. Milo *owns* them. I'm part of the reason he owns some of them, but there is always someone moving up in his ranks. Some of his girls like it. Some don't. But there are a few who thrive on it. The power they think it gives them with Milo."

"Where does he operate? Not in Evansville."

"No. He's mostly in New York. Sometimes he comes to Chicago."

"How did you end up here?" Eagle continued to question me. Though his expression bordered on furious, his fingers were gentle when they brushed a lock of hair off my face or wiped sweat from my forehead. He never raised his voice or swore. Not at all like the men I was used to being around.

"I-I got in trouble." I held back any tears of despair wanting to break free. Crying never fixed anything. Though I felt hopeless and like death was inevitable, I wasn't going to just roll over and take it. That's not how I'd survived all this time. Well, not really. I did what I was told, but I fought in my own way. Mostly just telling myself I did what I had to to stay alive. I'd hoped one day I'd have the opportunity to escape, but I think I'd given up on it ever coming. "I was somewhere I wasn't supposed to be and heard something I shouldn't have."

"Makes sense." Blaze leaned against the doorway his arms crossed over his chest. "Them idiots out there said they were supposed to show her what happened to whores who couldn't keep their mouths shut."

"They were going to kill me. I don't know if they were supposed to, but they were going to. I'm sure Milo wouldn't have cared, but he will care that I'm still alive and not under his control." I pushed up to stand. Eagle stood beside me and suddenly the room was too small. I pushed past Blaze and into the middle of the room, breathing deeply, trying to clear my mind of the panic trying to seize me. The room was too small for all the people in there. It was a tiny studio type apartment and there were six people besides me milling about. "I need some space." I opened the door and stood out in the hallway taking in big gulping breaths of air. Rose stepped into the hall with me but kept her distance. Like she knew how everything was crashing down on me.

"It's OK, Nyla," she said. "You're safe here."

"No. I'm not. Neither are any of you. If Milo finds out you're hiding me, he'll blow this place off the face of the earth."

"You let them worry about that." Rose said, emphatically. "Take some time to get your bearings. To rest in a safe place. You might find you like it here."

"Rose..." Atlas gave his wife a shake of his head.

"Stop it, Atlas. If she needs our help, she should be able to stay. No matter what the rules say. You can't turn her away. If Sting won't let her stay, I'll call my father. The Shadow Demons will gladly take her in."

"We won't turn her away, honey. But you can't expect her to consider something like this without knowing the score."

"Look," I said, wringing my hands in spite of trying to get a grip on my emotions and not to show fear to these people. "I appreciate the help, but I'd never be able to live with myself if he hurt anyone in this place because of me." I nodded to Rose's belly. "He'd kill your unborn child without a qualm. Just cut it out of you and watch you bleed out while you watch the baby die."

Atlas took a threatening step toward me, and I really didn't blame him. I couldn't stand my ground against the fury on his face either. "That's enough!" he snapped. "There's no reason to upset Rose. She's on your side."

"And I'm on hers," I countered. Finally, I found

my backbone. I was still intimidated to hell and back by these men, but I also knew the best way to get them out of this situation was for them to kick me out. "The very last thing I want on my conscience is the death of someone here. Especially Rose or her baby."

"Nyla. Stop." Eagle stepped into the hallway looking even more furious than Atlas. "You stay where the fuck you are."

I shook my head. "No. I really appreciate you helping me when I needed it, but I'm going to return the favor and leave. You gave me a fighting chance. The rest is up to me now."

"At least stay the night." Another woman stepped forward. I thought I'd heard someone call her Iris. Sting's woman. She arrived just as I'd come out of the bathroom. "Take a good soak in the tub, eat your fill, and sleep until you're rested. You can't run if you're exhausted. You'll make mistakes that could cost you your life."

As much as I hated to admit it, she was right. I was tired. Filthy. Hungry. And I had no way to survive on my own.

"You know she's right," Eagle said, taking a step closer to me. I met his gaze with a hard one of my own. I was still shaking with fear, and dread sat like a lead weight in my stomach, but I was trying to take charge of my situation. "Twenty-four hours. Give us that. If we can't find Milo or if it looks like things might get too hot to handle, I'll help you leave."

I narrowed my gaze at him. "That sounds suspiciously like a trap to me."

Eagle grinned. Too bad it didn't reach his eyes. He was dead serious. "No trap. Just telling you the conditions that need to be met for you to leave. If we haven't found Milo in twenty-four hours, you can leave. If we find him and the threat is too much for us to handle, you can leave."

"You sound far too confident for my liking. What do you know that I don't?"

"He knows that Iron Tzars MC is home to the motherfucking tech guy." A younger man with shaggy dark hair, with a bright green streak in it that fell across his forehead to cover one eye, approached us. He had a grin on his face and a tablet in his hand. "I'm Wylde, by the way. You Nyla?"

I nodded, not really wanting to answer him but knowing it was childish. "Um, yeah."

He handed the tablet to Sting as the other man stepped into the hall with the rest of us. I was starting to get claustrophobic again.

"Let's take this outside," Eagle said, moving toward me. He put his arm around my shoulders and urged me down the stairs at the end of the hallway and through the clubhouse. He didn't glance back to see if anyone followed, and he didn't let me slow down. Minutes later we stood outside in the moonlight. Stars were bright overhead and night bugs and frogs created a soothing din. I took a deep breath. Evergreen, hay, and the faint hint of gasoline filled the air. Off in the distance, I heard the rumbling of a motorcycle before it was shut off.

"I'm sorry if we crowded you, Nyla." Sting stepped onto the porch where Eagle had brought me. Eagle indicated I should sit on a wicker loveseat. It seemed out of place for a motorcycle club compound, but who was I to judge? When I sat, Eagle sat next to me, putting his arm over the back of the small couch behind my shoulders. A claiming gesture if ever there was on. Part of me wanted to cringe back, to keep him at a distance. The other part wanted to curl into him and let him keep me safe from anything and everything. If he would.

"I'm fine. But I really do need to go."

"You sure?" Sting asked. "Because if Wylde has found the right Milo, if he's found the man you're referring to, you're gonna need all the help you can get."

Chapter Three
Eagle

Nyla's face blanched which told the true story. She knew exactly how much trouble she was in, and she was terrified of this guy. Besides, Wylde was never wrong.

Iris stepped outside, bringing with her a huge plate of burgers. Winter followed her with a tray of fixings and Serelda with plates. Brick followed the women with a cooler of drinks, and everyone dug in. Nyla looked at us like we were all crazy.

"How can you sit here and eat calmly when you know who's after me?" She sounded equal parts incensed and horrified.

"Because this is what we do." Sting took a bite of his burger, giving her a wink. I thought it was meant to put Nyla at ease, but I wanted to point out to Sting he had his own woman to wink at. He kept it up. I might have to put out that eye. Then he'd have a reason to wink. As if I'd spoken aloud, Sting glanced at me with a raised eyebrow. Which was when I realized I was growling. The president smirked. Yeah. I was fucked.

"You absolutely stumbled onto the right group of people if you've got someone after you," Winter said softly. "We'll all defend you, but these guys take the protection of anyone in their territory seriously." Roman, as always, was by her side and kissed her temple. She'd stopped trying to hide her scars. In fact, she wore them proudly. Her badge of courage and sign of her indomitable spirit.

"And by this Milo bringing you into our territory for any reason, he brought you to us." Brick stood with his arms crossed over his chest looking every inch the vice president.

"That should tell you something," Nyla insisted. "If you've looked him up --" she nodded to Wylde, "then you know he's not some small-time thug. He didn't come here without knowing exactly who was in this area and what risk they posed to him. He obviously thinks he can handle any resistance to what he throws at you."

"No, he doesn't." Sting spoke quietly. "He has no idea we're even here."

That seemed to bring Nyla up short. Then she shook her head. "That's not... Milo is meticulous. He always knows everything about any clubs or gangs in the area. Normally he'd make his presence known so there were no misunderstandings."

"You seem to know a lot about him to not know his name." Roman spoke quietly. I looked over at him sharply.

"Roman."

He raised an eyebrow at me. "Well? You know it's the truth. I feel for her. I do. I want to help her and eliminate this Milo on sheer principle, but I don't like coincidences. She's here. In this compound. With a local MC that Milo Hutch, one of the biggest drug kingpins in the country, supposedly knew nothing about? Yeah. Not believing that. She's here for a reason. Whether she knows it or not."

I glanced at Nyla, who flinched. "You're not going to let me go. Are you?"

"All we're doing is lookin' into things." Sting raised a hand to keep everyone else quiet. "I'd be negligent if I let you go before we knew what was going on. But I promise, we're not going to hurt you. We'll protect you from Milo or anyone else as long as you're here in good faith. So if there's anything you need to tell us, do it now. Anything up to this point can be forgiven, even if you came here to deceive us and do something for Milo. Now's your one chance to come clean."

She shook her head. "I'm only here because I saw the lights when I escaped the house. You saw which way I came from. I ran straight to the lights."

"We've already backtracked you," Brick confirmed. "This was the only place anywhere close. We had cameras all over the area since it's just outside our compound grounds and the only other structure in the area not owned by us."

"I found where they brought in you and two other women." Wylde, usually the fun loving one always ready with a grin, was as serious as I'd ever seen him. "Found where they carried the bodies of the other two women out."

"I sent Walker and Cyrus in to scout out the place." Sting continued. "So far, everything you've told us, we've been able to corroborate with video and physical evidence. I'll know more when the boys get back from the property. I just need to know your story, Nyla. How did you end up with Milo and what was your function?"

She shivered and hunched in on herself. When she spoke, it was nearly a whisper. "I was a whore. He gave me to friends or associates. I was told what those men wanted and was expected to entertain them as they wanted me to. I also gathered information on everyone I slept with. That was my primary job, though the men he gave me to didn't realize it. That was part of the job. To not be noticed or looked at as a threat."

"How did you end up here?" Sting directed the flow of the narrative to get the information he was most concerned with.

"I-I overheard a conversation with Milo and a guy I was given to for the night. I don't know the guy's name, but he went by Dom. Milo mentioned another man named Claw, but I never saw him. I had no idea what they were talking about at first, but then I realized they were planning an auction. Of little girls and boys." Her voice broke and she bit back a sob. "There was a girl about twelve or thirteen in the room with them. She was naked but for her underwear, and Milo was about to make her take that off, too. I must have made a sound because both men turned to look straight at me." She swiped her hand under her nose as a tear tracked down her cheek. The longer she spoke, the paler she got. She seemed to be having a visceral reaction to the story and, honestly, I couldn't blame her. I felt much the same way. Worse, I thought I knew who this Dom and Claw were.

"Milo was furious. He dragged me into the room by my hair before calling in his guards. He gave me to them for the night. Told them they didn't have to be gentle. The next day, he brought me here. I don't even know where 'here' is. I was hurt worse than I'd ever been and couldn't concentrate on my surroundings even though he put me in his limo to bring me here. I thought it odd that he'd bring such a flashy car, but I was in so much pain, I couldn't really hold on to rational thought." She sobbed out the confession. "The guys he set to guard me -- Mick and Caleb -- were under instructions not to kill me, but anything else was on the table. The other two girls came a week later. They were there for Mick and Caleb to show me how bad it could get if I talked."

"Why not just kill you?" Sting asked bluntly. I wanted to throttle the younger man but settled for shooting him an annoyed look. My protective instincts were kicking in when I was never protective over a woman. I respected women. Was always careful of them as much as I could be physically. I was a surly, mean bastard on most days, but I kept to myself with the exception of being with my brothers. I still preferred to be alone. Which is why I often went hunting with Walker. Now that he had Blossom in his life, I tried not to rely on him so much. The brothers never let me go into the woods alone for extended periods of time because it never ended well. Though I felt better while I was out there, when they forced me back to civilization it was worse than when I left.

She shrugged. "I'm good at my job. He doesn't have anyone else who can get the information I can. There are women who are very good and one guy even better than me, but men aren't as useful as women, and I could get into places he couldn't."

Clutch, the club's road captain, shifted where he stood. "That good in the sack, huh?" His remark was said in a sneer, like he wasn't buying her story.

Nyla's face flushed a deep red. "I never said that. Just that I was good at getting the information Milo wanted."

"Don't like it, Sting." Mars, the bastard, never took his gaze from Nyla. "Smells funny to me. Especially since this Milo didn't even attempt to disguise who he was. He's close by. She likely knows where."

I was about to tell Mars to go fuck himself when Cyrus and Walker stepped outside. Both men were as stony faced as they came. Whatever they found at that shack wasn't good.

"Found one body and one they only thought was dead," Walker said without preamble. "Got her to Stitches, but he's not overly optimistic about her chances."

Nyla whimpered, wrapping her arms around herself. "Oh, God."

Walker nodded to Nyla. "Worried about that one. Said the boys were told not to kill her, but one of them had a thing for suffocating women while he fucked them."

Cyrus picked up the narrative. "Looked like that was how the one girl died. Strangulation. I'll leave it to Stitches to confirm, but it looked like she'd definitely had sex recently. Either unwillingly or she liked excessive violence."

"I thought they were both dead," Nyla whispered. "I should have made sure. Maybe I could have gotten her out with me…"

"Had a lot of time to plan your escape, did you?" I spoke softly, but insistently. There was no way I could let her take any blame for this particular fiasco.

She gasped and looked up at me. "It was only after I watched them… After… Mick untied me, getting ready to move me to the bed and chain me back up. Caleb was still with Leta. Jana… I watched him while he… Caleb slit Jana's throat while he…"

"That's pretty much what it looked like." Cyrus held Sting's gaze. "These guys don't appear to have any moral compass. I'll let Stitches make the final report to you, but it looked like she'd been murdered while she was raped, or immediately after."

Mars snorted. "Like you have a moral compass?"

Cyrus's gaze found Mars. "If I didn't, you'd have been dead a long time ago. Brother." Cyrus glanced at Nyla. "Not sure what she's told you, but I don't think any of this was staged. Course, if she's as good at getting information as she claims you should take that into consideration. And yeah. I heard most of what she said before we came out here. Also happen to think there's a good bit she doesn't know. Not and be beat up the way she is." He turned to go, then glanced back. "I'd make sure to keep her away from Mars, though. Given his lack of sexual partners, I'm sure there's a wealth of information she could extract from him if she's any good in bed."

As Cyrus had probably known it would, that got a rise out of Mars. He stood abruptly and took two steps toward Cyrus before Walker stepped between them and put a hand on Mars's chest. "Back off. He's baiting you. You know that."

"Fucker's askin' for it." If it were possible for someone to be so angry steam was coming out of their ears, Mars would've had it on full display. War and violence did funny things to a man. Mars often had violent flashbacks. As a result, more than one club whore had come out of his bed worse for wear. He didn't mean to hurt anyone, and every woman he took to bed knew the score and thought they could handle him. That wasn't who Mars was. He'd never hurt anyone on purpose unless they threatened his family. But because he couldn't always control his PTSD, he'd remained celibate for the past couple of years so he didn't accidentally hurt a woman again. I had no idea if it had helped or not, but he stayed clear of the women in and out of the compound. I could relate to Mars. It's what I often did when I'd been in any situation that might trigger me. Such as the run I'd just come back from.

Cyrus, though he had Asperger's and had difficulty relating to other people and their emotions, knew what he'd said would spear Mars. He also was aware enough to know Nyla hadn't deserved Mars's ridicule. So, Cyrus's remark was likely a punishment for Mars being a dick to Nyla. Which told me Cyrus was only an asshole when he wanted to be. Or didn't give a shit if people took him the wrong way or not.

"All right," Sting snapped. "Enough. Mars, stop being an asshole. Wylde, take Cyrus with you and do some computer shit."

Mars glared at Cyrus who just shrugged and left, turning his back on Mars without hesitation. That was who the Iron Tzars were. Mars and Cyrus might not see eye to eye, but they were both Tzars. They'd have each other's back even if they hated each other. Fights might break out at home, but no one was ever going to be out for more than a little bit of blood.

I leaned close to Nyla and murmured in her ear. "You're fine. Just take a deep breath."

"I'm so sorry. I don't want to cause problems."

"You're not." I let my hand find her shoulder and squeeze before putting it on the back of the wicker loveseat.

She looked up at me with wide, sad eyes. "Yes, I am. I'm a complication you guys don't need."

"Be that as it may," Sting interrupted, "you're staying here. At least for a day. Wylde and Cyrus will figure out what's going on with Milo Hutch. You'll get some rest and food. The old ladies will see to it you have some necessities, and you can have some peace and quiet."

"So, I'm a prisoner?"

Sting winced. "I prefer to think of it as us protecting you. Do you know how long Milo intended for you to stay with those two?"

She shook her head. "No. I mean, I never thought I'd be there as long as I was."

"Right. So if he comes looking for you, do you really want to be on your own? It sounds like you have a healthy fear of him already. Perhaps it would be a good idea to have some protection between you and him."

"Yeah." Nyla spoke softly. "I guess you're right."

"Eagle, can you take her back to her room and help her get settled? I'm sure she needs more to drink and something to eat." Sting raised an eyebrow at me. It was busy work, but he likely saw my interest in the girl. From the moment I caught her as she stumbled and fell, my protective instincts had been on overdrive. I supposed it was as good as anything else to keep me occupied and out of my head. Away from the violence I'd just come back from, even though it sounded like Nyla had come from a similar situation. Mars wasn't the only one with demons.

"I can. Also need to talk to you. 'Cause I think I have an idea who Dom and Claw are."

"Grim Road?" Sting raised an eyebrow at me.

"Yeah. They were with me on that last run. I'm guessing the conversation she overheard came in the middle of that operation. Either way, they'll have more info on Milo and his whereabouts."

"Also might explain why Milo chose to drop her here. Is it possible he meant to scout out Grim Road?"

"Possible, but I got no clue. Above my pay grade." I stood, extending my hand to Nyla. She looked at it for a long moment before sighing and placing her own small hand in mine. "Come on, girl. You need a proper bath and rest. I'll get you some food. Shoulda already eaten."

She went with me without protest as the conversation among the others continued. When we got back to the room she'd been assigned, I opened the door and let her proceed ahead of me. Instead of leaving, however, I intended to make sure she was taken care of.

"Go," I said. "Take you a shower, then I'll help you with your hair. It looks like a rat's nest."

Nyla nodded, her face flushing. "I'm not used to this. I was always supposed to be perfectly put together."

"No one can be perfect all the time." I tried to say the right thing, but I had no idea what the right thing was.

"You can if it's life or death." With that, she slid into the bathroom, locking the door behind her.

* * *

Nyla

There was no way I was going to survive here. It wasn't that I thought these people were going to hurt me or force me into a situation I didn't want, but rather that I might fall back into the role I'd been doing since I was a young teen. The short time I'd been here, interacting with the group, I could see similarities between the Iron Tzars and Milo's men. They were all hardened warriors. It was in every line of their bodies. The way they moved, watched their surroundings, listened to every single word that was said. It was second nature to them. I'd run away on instinct instead of thinking things all the way through. Pain and fear made me desperate. I needed to start thinking differently. Make a plan and stick to it.

I took my time, giving myself a thorough scrubbing and grooming. Underarms, legs, and privates all got a razor while I used the washcloth to scrub under my nails. My hair was a complete rat's nest. I was afraid the only way to get all the knots out would be to cut it. Of all the things to worry about, though, my hair should be the least, yet I couldn't help it. The need to look appealing was ingrained in me. It's what kept me alive.

Again, I exited the shower, much calmer this time. And more refreshed. My stomach was still knotted up, but I suspected that was as much from hunger as it was stress. My captors had fed me, but it had been mostly scraps and usually only once a day. Sometimes not even that. Most of all, I needed sleep.

I dressed in plain bikini panties, an oversized T-shirt, and a pair of cotton shorts. I had my hair in a towel with the brush I found in that backpack in hand. Eagle was sprawled out on a chair. He stood when I entered the room and moved to the refrigerator.

"What do you want to drink? I've got burgers and fries for your dinner. I can probably find something else if you don't like that."

"No. That sounds wonderful." I meant it too. Even soggy leftovers from some crappy fast food restaurant sounded like heaven right now. "Whatever you have to drink is fine."

"Soda, then." He paused, shaking his head slightly. "And some water. You probably need the water worse than a fuckin' soda." He muttered under his breath.

"I'm sorry to put you out so much." I felt horrible enough as it was. The last thing I wanted was this guy feeling like he had to babysit me. "You don't have to stay. I promise I won't go anywhere. You can even lock me in if you don't trust me, but you don't have to ruin your night by staying here with me."

Eagle turned from the fridge, his head whipping around in my direction. "What?"

I couldn't help my flinch. "I just mean that... You don't have to take care of me. I'll be fine on my own."

"Girl, I don't do anything I don't want to do. If I

didn't want to be here, I wouldn't be."

He turned back to the fridge and brought out a bottle of water, a pop, and a beer. I assumed the beer was for him, though I wouldn't mind having one. Just because I could.

I put my hands in my lap and waited for him to bring the food and drinks to the table. Looked like grilled burgers and homemade fries. He set my plate down and put the drinks between us and looked at me. I wasn't sure what he was waiting on, but decided it was for me to choose my poison. Naturally, I snagged the beer and popped the top before he could protest. Surprisingly, he just smirked before getting back up to get another beer from the fridge.

I took a swig and winced. I really hated beer, but by God, I was going to drink it. Wouldn't you know it, Eagle noticed.

"Drink what you want. You want to switch or drink all three, it's up to you."

"Who made the food?"

"One of the old ladies. Blossom, I think. She's a great cook and spoils us pretty badly." He didn't smile, but his tone was one of affection. "Eat up while it's hot. Her fries are pretty good."

Pretty good didn't even cover them. I'd never tasted anything so delicious in all my life! I started out a little hesitant. Last thing I wanted was this man seeing me devour a meal like I was starving. Even if I was. Three bites into the fries and one bite of the burger later, I couldn't have given a good Goddamn if he thought I was disgusting. The food was like ambrosia! The fries were perfectly done with the perfect amount of salt and grease, the burger thick, juicy, and loaded with the most wonderful cheese in the world. Even the beer started to taste exquisite.

Before I knew it, I'd eaten everything on my plate and trespassed on Eagle's. He didn't say anything, but scooted his beer over to me. I took it without hesitation. When it was all finished, I was full beyond belief. I sat back with a groan before looking up at Eagle.

Then the full impact of what I'd just done hit me.

"Fuuuuck..." I slumped down in the chair, resting my head on the back of it. "I'm so sorry."

"For what? Eatin'?"

"I ate everything on your plate too!" I snatched a napkin and wiped my mouth vigorously. Sure enough, it came back stained with grease, ketchup, and mustard. "I'm never living this down."

Eagle just shook his head and stood, bringing another plate from the bar at the small kitchen. "There's more. I brought enough for you to reheat tomorrow if you want."

"No. I feel like I'm about to explode."

He nodded. "I'll put this in the fridge, then. It's there if you get hungry again."

There was an uncomfortable silence. I wasn't exactly sure why it seemed uncomfortable other than Eagle seemed like he wanted to be anywhere but here.

"You don't have to stay with me, you know."

"You said that. You don't like my company?" The man could be so kind and gentle, but now he looked and sounded gruff and completely unapproachable.

"I didn't say that. You just seem... uncomfortable. Here. With me."

He looked away, shaking his head slightly. I'd noticed this gesture several times. Like he was about to do something he either didn't agree with or didn't like for some other reason.

"I'm not the most restful person to be around. None of us are. I want you to feel safe, but I don't want you to get the wrong idea."

I frowned. "What wrong idea?"

"That my looking out for you is anything more than protection. I don't expect anything else."

"Oh." I hadn't even thought of that. OK, I had thought about it, just not where Eagle was concerned. I had been drawn to him since the second I found myself in his arms. Not sexually, though, now that I'd had time to settle down and eat and start to feel human again, I could see how dangerously attractive he was. Had I met him at any other time in my life, I might have looked forward to the fun we could have together. But not now. Not after seeing me at my weakest.

"What I mean is, I've put you under my protection in the club. You chose me in front of Stitches, so he's backin' me up. You'll be staying with me while you're here. For as long as you're here." If it was possible for the man to look any more uncomfortable, he did. He stood and paced. "I'm not handlin' this right." He scrubbed a hand over the back of his neck. "Look. The club has rules in place regarding outsiders. We don't let them in without them knowin' what's expected and what rules they need to follow."

"I don't know the rules, but hopefully, I'll get to leave tomorrow and be out of everyone's hair. Until then, I can just stay in here. Right?" The spike of hurt in my chest because it was obvious he didn't want the job he'd been given surprised me. I didn't know this guy. Didn't know anyone here. "I didn't ask for you to stay, Eagle."

"You proved you trusted me to keep you safe

when Stitches raised his voice to you. That's what matters. We want you safe."

"I know I'm safe here. If you want assurances I'll stay in this room and keep out of trouble, you have them. Put someone outside the door if you have to, but please don't be miserable because of me. You don't deserve a duty you never asked for."

Eagle actually growled, turning his gaze to pin me where I sat. "You don't understand, girl. I've claimed you. You proved you were OK with the match back in Stitches's office. As of then, you're mine. The only thing I'm waiting on is for Wylde to come back with more stuff on Milo. Once we know where he is and what he intends to do, we'll know better how to move. But make no mistake, girl. You're mine. I don't let go of what's mine."

I blinked up at him, not understanding what he was saying. "You're going to have to explain this to me. Because it sounds like you intend for us to be together."

"I do."

"Then, why did you just say you didn't expect anything from me? If you intend for us to be together, then you clearly expect shit from me." I wasn't angry, just confused. "If I have sex with you, it will be because I want to. Not because you've decided to make me your woman or whatever."

Giving a crisp nod, like I'd confirmed exactly what he was trying to say, Eagle grunted. "Good. We understand each other."

"No, Eagle. We don't! Spell this out for me so I can understand. I'm not going to be with a man who treats me like property or doesn't like me for who I am. I also don't tolerate cheating. If I'm ever in any kind of relationship, it will be with someone who respects me enough to be faithful."

"I would be."

That prompted a sardonic laugh from me. "Right. Your sexually traumatized wife refuses to have sex with you, and you won't get laid somewhere else."

"No. I wouldn't." Eagle's expression was almost relaxed now. Like he heard exactly what he wanted to hear from me and was convinced I completely understood where he was coming from. It just made me that much more agitated.

"You expect me to believe that? I've never met a man who had no problem going without sex. Especially from his wife or girlfriend."

"I don't have sex much, Nyla. I get too rough. I don't want to hurt anyone." I scrubbed a hand over my face. "Couple of the brothers have the same problem. One of 'em's been completely celibate the last couple of years. I ain't that, but I can control myself enough to abide by your wishes."

"And you'd be OK with that?"

"If you don't want to have sex, I'm not going to pressure you. Didn't say I wouldn't try to tempt you, though." He grinned then, and he looked more like the man who'd rescued me at the gate and my stomach fluttered happily. When he truly smiled, the effect was devastating. Even though I never intended to give my body to anyone else ever again, I found myself getting aroused. Maybe sex wasn't completely off the table...

What? No! I was not even considering this!

"This is insane," I muttered. "I don't know you. You don't know me. We'd be divorced before the end of the first week."

"Don't believe in divorce. Besides, it's against club rules."

"What? Divorce?"

"Yep. 'Cause a man confides in his woman. Always happens. A woman gets mad at her man and leaves, she tells someone about her experiences. Good or bad. Private or not. Club secrets get spilled that way and puts us all in danger. So. No divorces."

"And if you abuse me? Hurt me? Degrade me?"

"You go directly to Sting, Brick, or Roman, or their old ladies. They'll take care of me properly."

"What does that mean?" My breath caught in my throat and I put a hand around my neck defensively.

"It means, any man in this club hurtin' a woman -- any woman, but especially his own woman -- is severely punished. If it can't be proven or if there is any doubt about what happened, you'd be given to someone else. Most likely to someone in a different chapter away from here. If not, if they believe I hurt you, I'd be dealt with." He held my gaze steadily. "Permanently."

I stood, pacing across the room, agitated but intrigued. And puzzled. "Why would you ever take a woman?"

"In this case, I'm doing it to keep you safe and trusting I can bring myself to be the man you need. I'll be a strong protector."

"You don't know me. All you know is that I might be some sort of spy for a known kingpin. Why would you put yourself in this position?"

"Honestly?" When I nodded, he continued. "I don't know. I'm not what you need, but I want to be. I don't know how else to put it other than that. Why?" He shrugged. "No clue. Only that I feel it in my gut. Have since I caught you in my arms outside the gate. You tellin' me you don't feel it too? Because I won't believe you. Not after the way you turned to me for protection and the way you let me take care of you when my club got to be too much."

"Look. I'll admit I seem to have latched on to you. Logically, I know it all started at the gate. You were my salvation, though I know you could have just as easily been my damnation."

"Never, Nyla. I'm not a good man. I've killed both for my country and my club. I'll continue to do so. But I'll protect you with my last breath. That means I have to kill a thousand men, that's what I'll do."

"I can't promise you I'll ever get to a point where I'll want sex. Not for a long while. So you better think carefully about this. Don't get yourself into a situation where you hurt us both."

He stepped close to me. Not getting in my personal space, but close enough I could smell the clean, fresh scent of his T-shirt and the distinctly masculine smell unique to Eagle. "Nyla, I can't explain why I need to be with you, I just do. There's something about you that... settles something inside me. I'm always at war with my memories and the present. When I'm around you, when I look at you even when you're not next to me, I feel a peace I haven't known since I was a kid."

"You've only been around me a few hours."

"And it's the only few hours in years I've not felt the urge to run away from everyone and everything and just be alone."

"You don't strike me as the type of man to run away from things. You fight."

Eagle nodded. "Usually. I just came off run with a club the Tzars have a loose alliance with. We help them out. They help us. I helped them take out a bunch of pedophiles. I'm not convinced Milo Hutch wasn't part of the ring we took down. I'm also not convinced that Grim Road isn't on to him. In fact, the man you mentioned you overheard talking to Milo is very likely part of that club. That's something Wylde is trying to nail down." He took one more step toward me.

This time, he was in my personal space, but I wasn't alarmed. I didn't feel trapped or cornered in any way. In fact, I slowly reached out and placed my hand on his chest. I could feel the breath moving through his lungs, his heart beating beneath my palm. The heat of him surrounded me, and for the first time in my life, I felt a connection with another person. As I gazed up into his eyes, I knew he felt it too. He didn't trap my hand against his body or pull me into his arms. Just gazed down at me, letting me feel the same thing he felt.

"Connection…" My whisper was soft. I hadn't even been aware I was going to say it.

"So you do feel it." Gazing up into his eyes, I nodded. "Good. Let me take care of you, Nyla. I swear you'll never regret it."

Chapter Four
Eagle

What the fuck was I doing? I couldn't take care of Nyla. Well, I could, but maybe not like she needed. She had gotten well and truly under my skin but good. It was the whole hurt female thing. She was fighting the only way she could -- by running -- and she'd run straight to me. As much of a hardass as I was, I absolutely could not stand to see a woman hurting. It was my weakness, but not a weakness I cared to rid myself of. Nyla might not have run to me intentionally, but I couldn't shake the feeling she was right where she was supposed to be. Run to me she did. And I intended to keep her.

I was serious when I told her I was claiming her. It was for her protection. So she'd have the whole club looking out for her and taking out anyone who tried to harm her. But it was more for me. I just plain wanted her. If she wasn't ready for sex, I was good with that. We'd figure it out. But I absolutely would not let her need to reclaim her sense of self-worth be a deterrent to her being with me. I'd do whatever I had to. And I had no idea why. I just knew I needed to protect her so that's what I'd do.

The next few days were awkward to say the least. Nyla didn't seem to know what to do with me, and I found it difficult to keep a comfortable distance away from her.

"You're creeping her out, man. What the fuck's wrong with you?" Blaze kept a close watch on her, too, which pissed me off something fierce.

"Ain't none of your business. All you need to know is she's mine. Keep the fuck away from her."

Blaze smirked, like he'd won a bet or something.

"Yeah, so I heard. You turnin' into a pussy or somethin'?"

"You sayin' those of us with women are pussies, Blaze?" Brick asked his question while cleaning under his nails with the tip of a wicked-looking knife. "'Cause it sounds like that's what you're sayin'."

"I'm sayin' he's followin' Nyla around like an overly aggressive Rottweiler. If she's his, he needs to figure out a way to be around her and not scare the bejesus outta her."

Brick nodded. "Point taken. He *is* rather bad at this stuff."

"You can both suck my dick," I groused, flipping them both off as I marched deeper into the clubhouse. Unfortunately, the two bastards followed me. Nyla was with Serelda and Winter at the playground the club was building for the children we'd amassed. OK, so amassed might be exaggerating a little. But there were several kids with us now. Most of them girls, and most of those were Sting and Iris's. With more on the way. Rose still had half her pregnancy to go, but they'd just found out she was expecting a girl.

"What's the world fuckin' comin' to when we have so many women and girls inside the club that ain't club whores? I hope you and Roman are makin' a pit to put the bodies of the boys tryin' to date any of them girls. Now I gotta figure out how to win mine over. It's all fucked up sideways and back."

Blaze let loose a guffaw while Brick laughed until he had to wipe tears from his eyes. "Life's definitely shapin' up to be interestin'. As to your own woman, give her some breathing room. She's been through a helluva lot." Brick managed to get out between bouts of laughter, the bastard.

"I know that," I groused. "But I can't seem to

keep my distance."

"Then go talk to her. Have a real conversation. She ain't gonna relax until she gets familiar with you, and that ain't happenin' with you staying just out of reach. Fuck, man! Ain't you ever talked to a woman before?" Blaze kept pushing while Brick's laughter picked back up.

"Sure, I have," I bit out. "Talked to hundreds of 'em."

"I ain't talkin' bout sex, Eagle. Though, Cyrus made fun of Mars, I hear from the club whores you ain't been around any of 'em in weeks."

"Longer than that," I muttered. "But that ain't no one's business but mine. I've had some shit going on and my mind ain't in the right space."

That sobered both men up. Blaze sighed as he scrubbed his hand with his face. "Sorry, brother. I know how that shit affects you. Why the fuck did you agree to go on that run with Grim Road? They had no right to ask you."

"No, but once they brought it to me, I had to go. Couldn't live with myself if I hadn't gone."

"And Rocket knows that and takes advantage of it." Brick was all business now. "It stops now. They have a noble cause and I'm all for helpin' out, but you can't be the one to go, Eagle. Not anymore. Especially not if you're serious about makin' Nyla your old lady."

"I am. And I know you're right. It brings the nightmares crashing around me. She doesn't need that."

"How you doin', by the way?"

I shrugged. "Nightmares are kinda rough, but I'm good. I stay far enough away from everyone not to get triggered until the whole thing fades a bit."

"Well, when you get your head right, you need

to tell her what the fuck's goin' on with you. She needs to know so she knows what to do if you go off."

"I won't be goin' off around her. 'Cause I ain't gettin' around her close enough to go off."

Blazed snorted. "Let me know how that works out for ya. You can't expect her to make any kind of commitment to you if you're never around her."

"She can't be around strange men much either, so it'll work out fine. We'll figure it out."

"This is a disaster waiting to happen." Blaze sat back in one of the chairs outside and crossed his feet where he propped them on the table. He laced his fingers together behind his head. "You better be ready if she runs, 'cause you only get one chance if she does." We had a good view of the women and the entire playground area under construction.

"I ain't claimed her yet. I put the word out she's mine, but we ain't made it official and Sting would never hurt a woman who didn't know the score. Not over something like this."

"He won't let her get hurt no matter what until she's in a better place. Serelda says she has trouble sleeping. When she does, she nearly always wakes up screaming less than an hour after she dozes off."

"I know. Been sittin' outside her door at night. One of the women always stays with her. They must rotate every night."

"They do," Brick said. "Serelda and Winter usually are the ones to stay. Said she thinks because they both wear the signs of their torture, that she can see the scars, especially those on their faces, that Nyla seems more comfortable with them. She feels like they know what she went through, though Nyla's scars are on the inside."

"Always amazes me how people don't

appreciate what they have. A good woman. Awesome kids." Blaze rarely expressed himself seriously except in battle, but the mistreatment of those who were so vulnerable was something none of us tolerated. For any reason. "I'll never understand how someone could hurt another person under their protection. Speaking of -- you heard from Wylde about that Milo character yet? He found anything on his whereabouts?"

"No," Brick answered. "But judging by the empty pizza boxes and Coke Zero cans in his office, I'd say he was up to his eyeballs in research. And, whatever you do, for God's sake do *not* open his office door. Not sure the man's showered since he started the hunt." That sounded like Wylde. When he was working like this, he was hyper-focused and the rest of the world could get fucked.

I made my way to Wylde's office. The women were occupied and watched closely by a couple of prospects, as well as Blaze and Brick, so I felt comfortable leaving Nyla. Barely. Knocking on the door lightly, I waited.

"What?" The question was a sharp bark. Obviously, Wylde didn't want to be disturbed.

"Just checkin' in," I said, not opening the door. Not only did I believe Brick about the state of our tech guy's office, but even though Wylde was the easy going one of the club, he had a darker side. Especially when he was hunting difficult prey.

"I'll fuckin' tell you when I fuckin' have somethin'. Go the fuck away."

All right, then.

"Grumpy bastard," I grumbled.

I was walking back down the hall to the back of the compound so I could keep Nyla in my sights when a deafening explosion rocked the building.

BOOM!

The clubhouse shook with the force, raining down plaster and dust. Wylde jerked open the door and tossed me a gun. He needn't have bothered. I was always armed, but when he was hunting this deep, Wylde was always armed and made sure everyone around him was armed as well. Wylde tracking prey we couldn't find always meant danger was close.

BOOM!

We stumbled as we ran through the clubhouse. "Nyla!" I yelled for her as I shoved open the door to the outside, needing to get to her. I could hear the women scream and the men shouting orders both to the women and each other.

I practically fell out of the door as another blast detonated. This time I saw two drones hovering overhead. One dropped something in the middle of the playground. Right next to where the women were directing the children to move out of the open and back to the clubhouse.

It seemed to happen in slow motion. I could see the explosive falling from the thing. Could see it was going to land in the middle of the women. I thought the kids were safely away, but I hadn't seen the other explosives land to know what kind of blast radius there would be, so I didn't know if they were far enough away.

"MOVE!" Sting's harsh command sounded just before the explosion detonated.

My gaze met Nyla's frightened one an instant before, then I was knocked off my feet and blown backward.

The next thing I knew I was gazing up at a smoke-filled sky. All around me urgent voices filled the air. The stench of ozone permeated everything, and debris rained down in a fine spray as the dust settled.

"Rose! Rose!" Atlas roared, his pain obvious. Rose had been with the other women. She was obviously hurt, but how bad? How bad were the others hurt? Nyla? Oh, God!

I scrambled to my feet and hurried to where bodies were strewn over the ground on the periphery of the blast. Some moved, others didn't. I saw Nyla struggling to sit up and skidded to a halt on my knees at her side.

"Nyla!" My roar was loud even to my own ears.

"I'm OK," she croaked. "The others..."

"I don't know, baby. Lie still. Help's comin'."

Seconds later, all the men were out in force, guns in hand. Shooter took aim at a drone leaving the compound and shot it out of the sky before trotting after it. Sting sat with Iris in his lap, rocking her even as he shouted out orders to the rest of the club. Blossom, Walker's woman, and Winter looked OK, but Serelda wasn't moving. Neither was Rose.

"The others..." Nyla gasped out. "I was standing right beside Iris..." She looked around until her gaze landed on Iris where Sting held her limp body.

Brick exited the clubhouse with an assault rifle and his handgun at the ready. "Serelda!" His roar filled the yard. His woman still didn't move.

The yard was filled with Iron Tzars members and prospects. A couple of the club whores were out too, armed just as much as the men. They wouldn't fight, but would be ready to help the men reload if necessary. We'd trained for this eventuality, but I never thought it was something we'd have to contend with.

"Someone get Stitches and Eagle!"

"I'm here," I called. Fuck! I didn't want to leave

Nyla, but she was at least conscious. "Don't you move. You stay right here, baby. Understand?" She looked up at me, wide-eyed, and gave a faint nod. "Good. I'm a medic and I have to help Stitches do a quick assessment of everyone."

"Go," she said. "I think Rose is really hurt. Serelda too."

I squeezed her shoulder gently and gave her a stern look. "Stay here."

I hurried over to Rose and Atlas. The big man had scooped up his pregnant wife and was heading inside.

"Stop!" I commanded the big man.

"She's not conscious!" Atlas shouted. "Need to get her inside to Stitches."

"I'm here." Stitches appeared beside Atlas and Rose, checking her pulse. "Put her down, Atlas. She doesn't have a pulse." Atlas looked like he was in shock, like he couldn't register what was happening. I couldn't blame him.

Stitches took the unconscious Rose and laid on her on the ground and started CPR. Always prepared, Stitches had his jump kit with him which I knew had an AED. While he worked on her, I hooked her up to the AED. While the machine was assessing her, I took time to set up an IV to push meds if we couldn't shock her out of it or if no shock was indicated.

"Fuck," Stitches muttered. "Gonna need to get her to the hospital."

The AED prompted us to shock her, thank God. That meant her heart was at least trying to work. "Stand clear." I made sure no one was touching Rose's body. "Clear... Shocking." I pressed the button and Rose's slight body twitched. Immediately, Stitches pressed his fingers to her neck.

"She's got a pulse. Get an IV started. Wylde, call EMS. I'm checking on the other women."

I did as Stitches instructed, glancing up every so often to make eye contact with Nyla. It didn't surprise that she didn't stay where I told her. She was up, checking on her new friends.

"Need someone over here!" she screamed, where she knelt with Brick and Serelda. "Now!"

Rose moaned and Atlas took her hand, kissing her fingers. "Atlas…"

"I'm here, baby. Help is on the way."

"The baby…" Her voice caught and her hands flew to her stomach. Atlas placed his big hands on top of hers.

"Don't," he growled. "Don't borrow trouble. We'll know after we get to the hospital and the doc checks you out. No way to check her now."

"I'm scared, Atlas. I don't want to lose the baby." Tears streamed down her face.

"Honey, I lost *you*." Atlas sounded gutted. "If we lose this child it will be horrible, but I can't lose you. I'll follow you if I do."

"Help's on the way," Wylde called.

"Eagle, how's Rose?" Stitches was working with Serelda who appeared to be unconscious."

"Awake and alert," I called back.

"Come to me. Bring my bag."

"Keep an eye on her, Atlas," I said, giving my brother a hard look. "Anything changes, even the slightest bit, you call out." Atlas nodded. I grabbed the jump pack and headed to Stitches.

Serelda was limp in Brick's arms. One side of her face was covered in blood and dirt with gravel embedded in the skin of her face and arms. Brick was stoic, but there was a tic in his jaw.

"Stitches..." His voice was gruff, belying his calm demeanor. "Help her."

"She's not dead, Brick. That's all I can tell you at a glance." Stitches was brisk, snapping when he normally would be trying to soothe. He glanced up at Brick. "When she goes to the hospital, I'll stay with her and the other women. You get with Sting and the others and find this motherfucker. You find him tonight."

"I'm not leaving my woman, Stitches."

"You are. All of you are. And you're gonna force the issue with the others. I'll take care of the women. It's what I do. You hunt this fucker and bring him to the barn. Then we'll all take him the fuck apart."

I could tell Brick was torn. He didn't want to leave Serelda to face her injuries without him, but he wanted this kill. Badly.

Nyla knelt beside Serelda and Brick. Tears streamed down her face unchecked. "Will she be all right?"

"Won't know until we get her to the hospital." Stitches continued to run his hands over Serelda, looking for more injuries. He cut off her clothing down to her underwear. There was a huge bruise in the middle of her chest and abdomen.

"Did you check on Iris?" Stitches didn't look up as he demanded the answer from Nyla.

"Yes. She was knocked out, but she's talking now. Answering questions appropriately. Bit confused and asking the same questions over and over."

Stitches just grunted. "I'll check on her next."

When Serelda moaned and her eyes fluttered open, Nyla let out a strangled sob. "Oh, thank God!"

"Hey, beautiful girl," Brick said, stroking Serelda's cheek gently with his thumb. "Look at me, sweetheart."

Serelda groaned in pain. "What the fuck happened?"

"We were attacked, baby," Brick said gently. "You're hurt."

"No shit." She pushed up to a sitting position, wincing as she did. "Where's Winter?"

"She's making sure the kids are all accounted for," Nyla answered. "She's fine. A little scraped and battered, but she's good."

"Iris? Rose?"

"You and Rose seemed to be hurt the worst," Stitches said. "Headed to check on Iris next, then I'm getting you all to the hospital."

Serelda's gaze darted around, probably looking for her sister. Then her gaze landed on me. "You make sure Brick and Sting hunt this fucker down, Eagle."

"Serelda --"

"No, Brick! I'm fine. And if I'm not, there's nothing you can do. What you *can* do is get after this guy." When he still didn't look convinced, Serelda shoved at his chest. "Go!"

"Fuck!" Brick curled his hand around Serelda's nape, leaning in to kiss his woman before putting his forehead to hers. "You better be all right or I'm gonna spank your sweet ass."

"I will be, and you can spank me anyway. Now go."

Brick met my gaze. "No mercy," he commanded. "We find this fuck, take him alive, and he pays. Slowly."

I nodded, my anger spiking. Someone had attacked the compound right under our noses. In our lair. As much as I needed to keep my distance, to find some inner peace so I could work on earning Nyla's trust, I had to take this up. Someone had to take the lead and since Sting, Brick, and Roman were too close, it had to be me.

Nyla looked up at me, her eyes wide. "I'm coming with you."

"Out of the question."

"You know this has to be Milo's doing. He's coming for me, Eagle. I'm not going to sit around and wait for him to make a play for me again, and I'm definitely not going to put anyone else in danger. If you won't let me come with you, I have to leave."

"Like fuck!" I grabbed her by the arm and dragged her toward the clubhouse. Nyla dug her heels in, pulling against me. Stopping, I turned and scooped her up over my shoulder and marched inside with her. I took her straight to my room before dropping her to her feet. "You'll stay here until I get back, girl."

"Just because you tell me to do something doesn't mean I'll obey."

"You will," I said, stepping into her personal space. "You'll obey me because when I come back you're going to be mine. I protect what's mine."

"I protect what's mine too," she fired back without hesitation. "We go together, or we separate for good. I won't be here when you get back."

"This guy will eat you alive, Nyla. You've been under his thumb. You know you can't take him."

"I can today."

Before I could form a reply, Nyla grabbed my beard and pulled me down for a scorching kiss. Her tongue thrust deep, but I could feel her hesitancy. Her body trembled in my arms where I held her against me. When she raised her hip to circle mine, when she made contact with my dick through my pants, I lost the ability to reason out why this was a bad idea. Instead, I gave her all the lust inside me, kissing her like I'd never kissed another woman. Because she was mine. I'd never let her go. It was time she realized that. Time we both did.

* * *

Nyla

For the very first time in my life, I got it. I understood what desire felt like. I'd been drawn to Eagle from the first, might have even been attracted to him sexually, but I'd never acknowledged it until now. My threat to leave if he didn't take me with him was as empty as the day was long because I could never leave him willingly. I'd fight by his side with my last breath.

This attack had proven to me how much these people had come to mean to me over the last few days. They were kind, supportive, and caring. Winter and Serelda had taken turns staying with me at night to help me through my nightmares. I knew Eagle was never far away from me. It was time I stood with them. Threw my whole self into this group of men and women because this was where I wanted to stay and try to make a home.

It didn't take long for Eagle to take the lead and I willingly followed. My leg was around his hip, and he gripped my bare thigh before sliding his hand under my cotton shorts to grip my ass cheek and squeezed.

"Fuck," he muttered between kisses. "Taste so fuckin' good!"

"Need you," I whimpered. "Need you inside me."

That seemed to bring him out of a daze and he pulled back. "I ain't like all the others, Nyla. I take you now, you're mine. Ain't no goin' back. You'll never leave me no matter what."

"I don't want to leave. This is where I want to stay. Always. With you and the others. But especially you."

"There's shit you have to know, and I ain't got time to explain it now." He lifted me, urging my other leg around his waist before carrying me to the bed. "You get this one chance to wait, girl. Otherwise, you'll take me and all the conditions that go with being part of this club, no matter what they are. You don't get to leave."

"Are you going to whore me out?"

"What?" He jerked his head back. "Fuck no! I'll kill any man who tries to fuck you! You're mine. I do *not* share. For any reason. *Ever!*"

"You gonna make me spy on dangerous people? Intentionally put me in harm's way?"

"Girl, I'm fixin' to spank your ass."

"Because if you have no intention of doing either of those things, then there's nothing that could make me want to leave you."

"I will always take care of you, Nyla. I'll protect you and keep you safe. Ain't gonna lie, I'm a gruff man. I have demons and a very dark side, but I'll never hurt you. Not intentionally."

I frowned. "But you would unintentionally?"

"I have flashbacks sometimes."

"Seems we have a lot to talk about." Again, I pulled him to me by his beard. He growled but kissed me again until we were both breathing hard. "Later. Now, I need you inside me."

Instead of saying anything else, Eagle set me on the floor and reached for the waist of my shorts, pulling them and my panties down in one swift tug while my fingers found the button to his jeans. He wore no underwear, so his cock sprang free the second

I had the button fly undone.

He was hard and thick, long. Before I thought about it, I dropped to my knees in front of him and engulfed him, taking him deep and swallowing to massage the head of his dick.

"Goddamn!" He fisted his hands in my hair as he tilted his head back. The tendons stood out in his neck, making the tattoos creeping up the side dance before my delighted gaze.

Lust rode me hard. All encompassing. I needed to please this man because I knew he'd return the favor, but also because I loved the expressions on his face. The unchained lust as I pleasured him.

I'd seen the look more times than I cared to admit, but this time was different. Eagle looked helpless to do anything other than let me suck his cock. Occasionally he'd tug at my hair like he was going to pull me off him, but never committed to it. When he looked down at my upturned face, he looked almost shell-shocked. Like I'd gotten one over on him and he wasn't sure what to do about it.

"Girl, stand up. Now."

I didn't. Instead, I sank my mouth deeper around him. His thick girth stretched my mouth uncomfortably, and I might have scraped him with my teeth more than once. Not that he seemed to mind. In fact, every time I did, he shivered and his grip on my hair tightened. And his dick let go of a little precum.

"Goddamn it, Nyla! Fuck!"

"Mmm…"

The vibration around his cock must have set him off because Eagle gripped my hair and fucked my face hard and fast. As he looked down at me, he seemed helpless and horrified by his actions. Like he wanted to ease up but had no strength to do so. I gripped his ass, pulling him to me in encouragement, to let him know the only way I could that I wanted this. Needed it, even. That seemed to be the last thing he could take. With a brutal roar, Eagle came down my throat. The muscles of his arms strained the fabric of his T-shirt and the grip he had on my hair was an erotic bite.

The second he finished, he pulled out and yanked me to my feet by my hair, fusing his mouth to mine. There was no doubt he could taste his release on my tongue, but he didn't seem to care. One arm wrapped around me, holding me close to him as his kisses continued to scramble my brain.

"Ain't got time to do this proper, but I can't wait one more second to be inside you, girl."

"Yes," I breathed out. Surprisingly, his cock was still rock hard and throbbing where it was mashed between us. I shivered in anticipation, reaching between us to stroke him.

"Fuck!" He leaned in to catch my neck with his mouth, biting sharply as he lifted me back into his arms, pulling one thigh around his hip. I followed with my other leg and shifted until the head of his cock was at my entrance. "Once I do this, that's it, Nyla."

"You said that. Stop stalling and fuck me already!"

With a grunt, he thrust his hips, impaling me on his thick erection. It was a tight fit, but the burn was as erotic as the whole situation. I loved the bite of pain, the rough way he handled me.

When he started moving, I let my head fall back and moaned in pleasure. This was new. I'd never felt pleasure during sex. Keeping my wits about me had been something Milo had drilled into me from the first. Sex had never been about pleasure. Never about fun or expressing love. It was a means to an end. Not this time.

"I'm gonna take care of you, baby. Always. You get me?"

"You already are, Eagle. Never... I've never... God! Feels so good!"

"Mother fuck!" He shook his head hard, like he was trying to regain the control he'd lost. "You're gonna have to explain, girl."

"I've never felt like this," I gasped out. "It's right there! So close but..."

He moved to the bed and lay down on top of me, never separating our bodies. Shifting so that he was more firmly against me, his cock going impossibly deeper, he started a hard-driving rhythm. Each thrust put friction on my clit that hadn't been there before. Each time his body rubbed against me, pleasure zinged through me until I was on the precipice of something extraordinary.

"Eagle! OH, GOD!"

"That's it, honey. Just let it happen. Come for me."

As if he'd flipped some kind switch inside me, my lower body spasmed, contracting in some kind of painful pleasure I'd never experienced before. The rest of my body soon followed, tightening and contracting, forcing a guttural scream from my throat. I clung to Eagle, afraid to let him go. Afraid he'd leave and take this wonderful pleasure away and never bring it back.

All too soon, the sensations faded leaving me drained and sleepy. Satisfied beyond measure.

"Holy shit..." I thought I might pass out right here without moving. I lay limply as Eagle sped up his movements, burying his face in my neck and groaning. I felt him release inside me, his warm seed bathing me inside.

"Fuuuuck..." He shuddered, licking and nipping my neck as we both came back to ourselves. Eagle raised his head, looking down into my face. He stroked hair off my damp forehead gently. "I'm sorry, honey. Was I too rough?"

"You were exactly what I needed. Eagle... that's the first time I've ever..."

"Come?" When I nodded, he gave me a soft smile, leaning down again to give me a soft kiss. A warm and fuzzy pleasure poured over me. Like the lethargy that follows a high. "Baby, I swear I'll always give you as much pleasure as I can. Always." He kissed me again, a sweet, gentle brushing of his lips and tongue before pushing himself off me.

Lifting me into his arms he carried me to the bathroom where he set me on the wide vanity and cleaned us both. Then he wedged his hips between my legs and gripped me behind my neck, looking into my eyes.

"I need to go hunting. This is what Iron Tzars does."

"I understand. Give me five minutes to get dressed."

"No, honey. I need you to stay here. Really need it. I can't have you in any more danger today and I'm afraid if you come with us, my attention will be focused on you and your safety instead of on the task at hand. It could get us all killed."

"Oh. I hadn't thought about that." I looked away, but he gripped my jaw with his other hand and turned me to face him once again.

"I need your word you'll still be here when I get back. I'm serious when I said I wasn't letting you go. You're mine now. No taking it back."

I nodded. "All right. I won't leave."

He grunted, stepping back. "Good."

"Is it OK if I go with the other women to the hospital? I could look after them. I'm sure Stitches could use another set of eyes with so many of them hurt. Especially Rose." Everything came crashing back, hitting me hard. "Oh, God! What are we doing? Having sex while Rose and Serelda are so hurt?"

"Hush, girl," he snapped softly, kissing me again. "We needed to get this settled between us. I promise you, none of them are going to think badly of you for this. Of either of us." He sighed. "Iron Tzars is different from a lot of MCs, Nyla. I don't have time to explain things to you yet but trust me when I say, we needed these few minutes to set our expectations for each other. For the record, though, I never expected you to have sex with me. I'll never expect it, but I will try to coax you into it." He gave me a wicked grin, and I couldn't help but smile. "So, yes. Go with Stitches and help take care of the other old ladies. They can answer any questions you don't want to wait on answers for. Anything else, I'll explain when this is over."

"OK. Good." I slid my arms around his neck and clung to him. "Thank you, Eagle."

"Owen," he said gruffly. "Owen Asher."

"I suppose it's something we should know about each other, huh. My last name is Pippin."

"Not for long," he growled, then gave me another hard, quick kiss. "I have to go. You're to stay with Stitches or the other patched members at the hospital. Do not go off by yourself. If this attack was about revenge on you, you're not safe. The hospital will be the safest place for you until we get things taken care of here, but you are not to go anywhere alone. Get me?"

"Are you always so bossy?" I was amused and

knew he could tell when he scowled at me, pointing a warning finger at me.

"Always. And you'll do what I say."

I gave him a crisp salute even as my lips twitched. "Sir, yes sir!"

"Brat." He helped me down and we both dressed.

By the time we left his room, the rest of the club had prepared for the hunt. I'd never seen so many big, scary guys with big, scary guns in my life. Even Milo's men didn't look as dangerous as these guys. Probably because they were a unit, a band of brothers, while Milo's men were all out for themselves. I had the impression that these guys would fight to the death for what they believed in. I knew for a fact that Milo's men were there for the money and nothing more.

We met Sting in the common room where everyone was packing weapons and ammunition. "You two get things settled between you?" He looked from one of us to the other. I probably should have been embarrassed to think Sting knew what we'd done, but I wasn't. Instead, I only felt supreme satisfaction.

"We did," I said before Eagle could. "He says there's still things I need to know, but I'm not leaving him."

Sting gave a short nod. "Good. He needs you, Nyla. You take good care of my brother."

"You have my word," I said solemnly.

"Shut the fuck up, Sting," Eagle grumbled. "I'm the one takin' care of her. Not the other way around."

I wanted to grin but managed to hold on to my smile. "We'll take care of each other. Because that's what mates do."

Sting grinned. "Yep."

"Everyone ready?" Eagle pulled me to him, kissing my temple. Like we'd been together forever. It melted something in my heart as nothing else ever had before.

"We are," Sting said. "Puttin' Clutch in charge of this one, brother. Pretty sure this is about your woman, and the rest of us have an ax to grind. Clutch is the highest rankin' officer with combat experience and no personal stake."

Eagle nodded. "I'm on board with that. Who's at the hospital with the women?"

"Stitches, obviously. Mars and Ace. Wylde is staying here to monitor everything. I think the fucker managed to hack into the city camera system and has eyes everywhere."

"Good." He turned back to me, cupping my face between his hands. "You promise to stay with one of them at all times." It was an order.

"I promise, Eagle. I'm not going anywhere and I'm not going to put myself in danger needlessly."

"At all, girl. You won't put yourself in danger at all."

I smiled. "You know I'll also protect my new friends, right?"

"Girl…"

I kissed him. "Go. Take care of business and come back to me. We have a shit ton to talk about."

"That one's gonna be as big as a handful as Winter and Serelda ever thought about being." Sting seemed amused but Eagle just scowled.

"Don't encourage her, Sting. She's not as fragile as I first thought and I'm not sure I like this courage she has."

Sting laughed, clapping Eagle on the back. "Welcome to the club, brother."

"What club? The one where every woman in the place takes our man cards?"

"Exactly."

Chapter Five
Eagle

Wylde came through in brilliant fashion. "If I've never told you before you're the motherfucking tech guy, Wylde, I'm telling you now," Clutch muttered through his throat mic.

"Unsolicited praise is unneeded but always welcome," Wylde's chipper voice answered. "These guys are sophisticated but stupid as shit."

"You sure these are our guys?" Brick asked, his voice soft but no nonsense. He didn't take his eyes away from the night vision field glasses where he studied the house Milo Hutch's men had set themselves up. "They seem a little relaxed for what they did this afternoon. Not like they expect anyone to come after them."

"They think they got away clean," Wylde said. I could hear him popping his gum. He was decidedly more relaxed now that he'd found his prey. "I can hear them laughing about how they got the drop on us with that drone. Think we couldn't use it to find them."

"I thought you used the city camera system to find them," Clutch commented.

"Nope. Shooter recovered a drone, and I backtracked the remote signal."

"I'm assuming you also hacked something inside the house to know what they're talking about."

"Please," Wylde scoffed. "Why would you even consider I wouldn't hack into the house? You know. Phones. Computers. The security system. Anything hooked to a router or any network including satellite. Which they have, and think is secure." He popped another bubble.

"Why indeed," Clutch muttered. "Sound off."

This time his voice was stronger, a commander expecting obedience. Every member of the team signaled their readiness. "Remember, no one dies."

"Yet," I muttered, which got a few chuckles.

"Right. Let's do this."

Gaining entry to the house was nothing. Me and Cyrus kicked in the door while the others took various windows. Ten minutes later, the whole group was on their knees, bound and gagged, looking as shocked as anyone could. It was almost comical.

"Well, that was anticlimactic," Clutch muttered. "They get off a message to Hutch?"

"Nope," Wylde answered. "I hit all their electronics with a bit of a surge, you could say."

"Huh?" Sting's brows knit together.

"Little something I modified from Argent Tech. Need-to-know only."

"Cocky bastard." Clutch shook his head, but he grinned.

"It's only being cocky if you can't back it up. And I'm the motherfucking tech guy."

We loaded everyone up. There were six of the bastards. We stripped them down and secured them in one of the trailers we'd normally use to haul our bikes. They'd be entering our compound naked as the day they were born, which would delight the club whores to no end. It was all part of the torture, mental rather than physical. They had answers we wanted and, with what they'd done to our women, they didn't get to keep any dignity.

"Take them to the barn. Put them in the stall across from Maniac and Lynch." Sting was now firmly back in control. He'd relinquished it for this op to keep from getting anyone killed if things went sideways since his instinct would be to go after the fuckers no matter what, but I'd known he couldn't last long.

"You killin' those two tonight?" Brick asked the question, looking eager. Maniac and Lynch had been lingering for a couple of months now. The pair had betrayed the club by trying to oust Sting as president in a less than honorable way. If they'd been successful, Brick and Sting would both be dead. They were paying for their actions now.

"It's time. Besides, killin' those two in front of these fuckers should get the point across we mean business. Save some time." Sting stood outside the trailer while Clutch opened it. A couple of the men inside grunted but otherwise said nothing. I almost smiled at the defiant looks thrown our way.

"These pissants have no idea what's about to happen, do they?" Roman chuckled. "Will make the next few weeks interesting."

"Weeks?" one of them squeaked.

"Shut up, Brody. Not a fuckin' word." The other guy growled his command. Probably the leader. Without even trying, we now knew the weakest and the leader of the group.

"Oh no," Clutch said, raising his eyebrows. "By all means. Keep talking. Especially if you want to beg. We'd like to hear that."

"So would our women." Brick's voice was as deadly as ever. "Since they're the ones you hurt."

A couple of them exchanged looks. "We don't hurt women or children," one of them said. "The drone was placed carefully in an area where only club members would be. We were assured of the position."

Brick snorted. "Not sure who told you that, but they're a Goddamned liar."

"Or incompetent," Wylde added as he approached, obviously hearing part of the conversation. He had a wide grin on his face. "Personally, I'm going with both." His grin said he knew that for a fact.

"We took this job with the understanding we were going to retrieve property of our boss. He said nothing about harming anyone other than the bastards who took that property in the first place. We were told to deliver the warning, then hole up until he gave us instructions."

"So, you're not part of his syndicate?" Sting asked.

"We're mercenaries."

Brick sighed. "Always with the fuckin' mercs. Are all y'all stupid or somethin'? Is it a requirement to be a merc? When someone like Milo Hutch hires you for a job, it's a suicide mission. He has his own fuckin' army of men who could have done this."

"Fuckin' bastard," the guy grumbled. "I get we're toast and I ain't in no position to make requests, but if you happen across that bastard, shoot him for me, will ya?"

"I could almost feel sorry for these guys." Roman shook his head.

"Their boss said they were free game. Apparently, the six of 'em are expendable." The news was delivered gleefully. "Also, I know where that fucker is, Sting. Put some measures in place to keep him there until you decide how you want to proceed. Take as long as you want. He won't be going anywhere."

"Oh?"

"Yep. Feds have been looking into him for the usual mob shit. I called in a favor. He'll be arrested tonight and held without bail for the foreseeable future."

"That won't hold him long," I said, scrubbing a hand over my face. "A week? Two?"

"Oh no. It's amazing what can happen when your file gets buried in a database somewhere. I basically tossed him in a hole and threw away the hole." Wylde grinned like he thought he was clever.

"You've been watching too many Goddamned movies," I grumbled. Wylde was brilliant, but he was also an asshole.

Wylde just shrugged. "Shame to waste a good movie line, especially since it's true. Milo will remain in solitary confinement until you're ready to deal with him, Sting. His lawyers will make a fuss, but the paperwork has been lost and he's not showing in the main database. The only people who have access to him don't know there's an issue and I'm intercepting all communication regarding Milo."

Brick shook his head. "He's too high profile a prisoner to keep him hidden for long."

"Trust me on this, boss. He's not going anywhere."

"Good." Sting clapped Wylde on the shoulder. "Good work. Cyrus, take Blaze and secure these fucks. Clutch, you're in charge. Anyone needs me, I'll be at the hospital with my woman."

Cyrus got all the men out of the truck, tying them together like prisoners on a chain gang. Not only were they naked, but barefoot as well. Walking on the gravel in their death march added insult to injury. To their credit, only one of them wasn't stoic about it. But really. Gravel on bare feet was its own torture.

Thank fuck Sting was letting us go to the hospital. I wasn't sure how much longer I could stay away from Nyla. She was all in when I left her, but I was afraid that if I gave her too much time to think about it, she'd balk. Which wasn't happening.

"Any update?" Brick looked pointedly at Wylde.

"Only that everyone's alive. Stitches says he's most concerned about Rose. She seems OK, but they're still trying to determine how the baby's going to do. Not sure when she'll be able to come home."

"Atlas?"

"He's a wreck," Wylde said. "Hasn't left Rose's side. Which leads to the next problem. Alexei Petrov has arrived at the hospital, so everyone's scrambling to make sure the women have everything they need. I seriously doubt he lets Rose stay where she is much longer. He'll likely bring in his own people to manage her care."

"Take advantage of that shit, Sting," I interrupted. "Get him to make sure all the girls are taken care of."

It was Wylde who answered me. "Already taken care of. Rose didn't even have to bully him into it. According to Stitches, she insisted the second he walked into her room, even before reassuring him she was OK. Your woman also had a hand in it, Eagle. She's been with Rose the entire time, only leaving to check on Serelda and Iris from time to time. When Alexei got there, she immediately involved him in everyone's situation, not just Rose's. Obviously, Rose was just as adamant. From what Stitches said, once Nyla found out Alexei had practically unlimited resources, she made a list of what everyone needed, including private physicians and comfortable beds instead of crappy hospital beds. She's a regular little drill sergeant. You'll have to get Merrily to tell you all about it. She's getting a kick out of the way Nyla is 'directing traffic,' as she calls it."

"Guess that answers the question of if your

woman's gonna stay," Sting said with a grin. "You explained things to her yet?"

"Ain't had time. She knows I'm not lettin' her go, but she doesn't know the full extent of it. Give me some time to let things settle down here, then I'll get Ace to do her tatt."

"Sure she'll be good with that?"

I shrugged. "I think so. Once I explain how we're all inked. I'll follow everyone else and get my own property patch in the form of a ring tattoo."

"Wise choice," Brick grunted. "Now if we're done chitchatting, I need to get back to my woman. If Alexei Petrov is there, I'm going to try to get him to bring everyone back to the clubhouse except Rose. Sounds like she has a rough road ahead."

"OK. Anyone here, make preps in case we get things worked out at the hospital. I want the club whores confined to quarters until this is all worked out. Last thing we need is one of them thinking she can sink her claws into Alexei Petrov. Not sure how his wife Merrily would take it, but with her computer skills, I'm sure she can cause no end of problems."

I didn't wait to hear anything else. Five minutes later, I was on my bike, headed to the hospital. And my woman.

* * *

Nyla

"I'm just saying, everyone but Rose would benefit from being taken care of at the clubhouse, Mr. Petrov."

"You said that, Nyla. Several times."

"And I'll keep saying it until you do something about it!" I was pushing it. I knew that. I also knew Alexei Petrov wasn't a man I should push.

"I bet if you hired the right people and brought in the right equipment, even Rose would benefit. I know she needs special monitoring and facilities in case the baby has difficulty, but she'd be so much more comfortable both mentally and physically if she were in her own home."

"Girl, back off." His voice was calm, but the expression on his face told me he was done dealing with me. Yeah. Seen that look before.

"I will not," I snapped. "These women are my friends! I will do whatever I have to do to take care of them."

Petrov opened his mouth to reply, but Atlas stood and moved in front of me. "You've already made plans to do exactly what she's suggesting, Alex. Stop baiting her."

"What?" Confusion warred with anger. "If you planned on doing that all along, why didn't you just say so?"

Petrov looked at me coolly. "Because you don't give orders to me." The menace in his gaze had me stepping back, my hand going to my throat defensively.

"Dad, stop it!" Rose cried. "Nyla's a good person and looking out for all of us."

"She needs to learn she doesn't always get her way."

"Always get my way?" Pushing past Atlas, I marched up to Petrov. Before I could think better of it, I slapped him. Hard. "Always get my way? You know nothing about me, you bastard! I haven't had a choice in life! Never! Not until I met these people. You might be all rich and righteous, but you're just like all the other men I've been given to. You think I always get my way? When was the last time you *didn't* get your way?"

"What's going on?" A woman I hadn't met stepped into the room.

"Mom, Dad's being a giant dick." Rose sounded pained. I turned to look at her, and her hand clutched her belly. Sweat dotted her forehead. Her gaze found Atlas and tears filled her eyes. "Get the doctor, Atlas."

"Oh, God." I hurried to Rose's side. She reached for my hand and her grip was punishing. "Rose!" Atlas hurried out and I pressed the call button on the side of the bed. "Atlas will get help. He'll fix everything."

"I don't think he can fix this, Nyla." Tears tracked down her face as she looked at me. There was a sad acceptance in her eyes that hurt so bad.

"This is my fault," I whispered. "If I hadn't stayed --"

"You'd have been killed," Rose interrupted. "And I wouldn't have found such a wonderful friend."

Rose's mother had a wet cloth she gently brushed over Rose's face, clearing the sweat from her brow. "Baby..."

"I'm scared, Mom." Rose's whispered confession tore lose a sob from me.

"Baby, I'm sorry. If this is anyone's fault it's mine. I should have protected you better and I shouldn't have upset you."

"How about we put the blame where it belongs," Atlas said as he entered the room with Rose's doctor. "Milo and those mercs he hired."

"Did your club find everyone?" Petrov asked the question even with the doctor in the room, which meant either he was careless or stupid. My eyes widened and I looked at Rose who smiled at me despite the pain she was going through.

"Don't worry. Viggo is part of Shadow Demons."

She gasped in a breath at the end, her hand tightening around mine even more.

The doctor was followed by a tech who rolled in an ultrasound machine. He raised Rose's top and squirted some jelly before putting the probe gently on her skin and moving it around until he saw what he wanted to see. The longer he worked, the deeper his frown. Atlas was on Rose's other side, kneeling beside her, holding her hand to his lips. They looked at each other as if they were speaking. Atlas was calm but reassuring. Rose was terrified.

"I'm sorry, Rose," was all the doctor said. He kept moving the probe, though, shaking his head and flipping switches and stuff on the machine. It was as if he were willing the device to show him something -- anything -- other than what he was seeing. "I'm sorry. We did all we could, honey."

She gasped out a sob and dissolved into tears. Surprisingly, she kept her grip on my hand even if her attention was focused on her husband.

"I'm so sorry," I whispered, raising her hand to my lips to kiss her fingers gently.

When I stood, she tightened her hand farther. "Don't go yet, Nyla." Though tears clogged her throat, the order was clear.

"If you want me here, Rose, I'll stay." I glanced up at Atlas who gave me a nod and a slight smile, letting me know I made the right choice.

It wasn't long before a team of people came into the room, explaining to Rose what was about to happen. I couldn't process any of it, only that my friend had lost her baby. And I had a part in that happening.

As if she could hear my thoughts, Rose turned her heat to me. "Don't, Nyla." She was fierce. "This is not your fault. Don't you dare leave because of this. Eagle needs you. I need you. You're my best friend!"

That shocked me. Sure, Rose and I had connected that first night, but did she really see beyond my past and what I was forced to do?

"I'm not sure that's the best thing."

"Promise me, Nyla. You'll be here when I -- when this is over."

I knew I needed to save these people. To get away. But I also knew I'd never abandon Rose. "All right," I whispered. "I promise." That seemed to make her feel better. She gave my hand one final squeeze before the nurses rolled her out of the room. Atlas followed, as did Alexei and her mother.

For a long while I sat in Rose's room, replaying everything in my head since the moment I first stumbled into Eagle's arms. These people had become my family. At least, that's how I thought of them.

Standing, I made my way to Serelda's room. She was demanding to know what was going on with Rose. The nurse at her bedside taking her blood pressure firmly but gently told her she couldn't give out patient information. I stepped into the room and Serelda's gaze landed on me. We didn't speak, but Serelda's face crumpled and she broke down into tears.

"Is Rose going to be OK?"

I shrugged helplessly. "I don't know. I think so, but the doctor didn't actually say. I don't think they were able to save the baby, though again, he didn't actually say. They're taking her off now. I think to surgery."

The nurse finished and I pulled a chair next to Serelda's bed. She held out her hand and I took it. "Don't even think about leaving us, Nyla. You're one of us now. We protect our own."

"I promised Rose I'd be here when she got back, but I really think it would be best if I didn't stay after that. All I've done is bring trouble to your door."

"You try to leave and I'll stop you." The gruff growl came from the doorway and Eagle stepped through, followed by Brick.

I jumped up and flung myself into his arms. All the fear and tears I'd been holding on to exploded out of me in a rush. The only thing that held me together, that kept me from completely shattering was Eagle's strong arms and soft words in my ear. I had no idea what he said to me, but the sound and his scent were comforting.

I have no idea how long Eagle held me or how long it took me to calm down, but once I did, I heard Serelda's soft voice. I thought she was updating the guys on what had happened since she'd gotten to the hospital, but I wasn't sure.

"I need to check on Iris," I said into Eagle's chest.

"Take her, Eagle," Serelda said. "I'm good with Brick here. Did Sting come with you?"

"Yes. He's with Iris now."

"Good. Take Nyla to Iris, then get her home. She needs looking after and loving care."

"I shouldn't stay," I whispered. "What if Milo tries for me again?"

"Don't worry about that bastard," Brick said, briskly. "He's been taken care of."

That brought me up short. "Taken care of? Like for good?"

"Mostly," Brick said, shrugging. "He will be, though. And he's contained. He won't be hurting you or anyone else ever again. When he dies will depend on how cooperative he is."

"You make that bastard suffer." I didn't mean for

that to come out as an order, but there wasn't much I could do to hide it.

To his credit, Brick just nodded. "I promise."

We checked on Iris. Sting was sitting on her bed, holding Iris in his lap. She clung to him but seemed otherwise not in distress.

"Thank you for keeping an eye on our women, Nyla. Iris says you were a great comfort to all of them."

I blinked in surprise. "Really? I was afraid I was in the way, but I couldn't leave everyone alone. They're my friends. I've never had friends before."

"You have a whole club full of them now, honey." Eagle spoke gently. "You never forget that. They don't love you because you're my woman. They love you because you're *you*. Pretty sure most of them would take you over me any day of the fuckin' week."

"That's because you're generally grouchy and a pain in the ass," Sting said cheerfully.

Iris and I shared a grin before we both started crying. Eagle let me go to her and I hugged the other woman as fiercely as she hugged me.

"Rose will need us, Nyla. You remember that when you try to talk your man into letting you leave. Rose needs us. All of us. You most especially."

"I think I need her too," I acknowledged softly. "I need all of you."

"Good." Iris sniffed and smiled at me through her tears. "Because we all need you, too."

Eagle urged me gently from the room and took me outside the hospital. I took a deep breath of air. "I didn't realize how claustrophobic I'd gotten until just now."

"Are you sure you're not hurt, honey? You got checked out. Right?"

"Atlas insisted. And yes. I'm fine. I'm sure I'll be

sore tomorrow. I got knocked on my ass. But I'm not injured. It's Rose who was hurt the worst." Just the thought of her losing her child cut me like a knife, the pain nearly doubling me over.

"She's tough. This will hurt, but she won't lay down and quit. She'll grieve and we'll all be there to help her. But she's strong. She wouldn't be Atlas's woman if she weren't."

She was silent for a moment before she spoke again. "I got tested. You know. While I was there. I'm clean even though sometimes the men I was with didn't use protection. Milo gave me an implant to prevent pregnancy and I had it removed. It's not that I want to get pregnant right now. I just…"

I finished for her, knowing exactly what she was getting at. "You didn't want anything left of Milo in your life."

"Did you find the men who did this?"

"Wouldn't be here now if we hadn't. It's all taken care of."

"What about Milo?" I cringed when I asked. Even saying his name made me want to vomit.

"Taken care of. He's not dead yet, but he will be. After a while."

"He's dangerous, Eagle. Don't play around with him."

"We're not. Wylde is keeping an eye on him, and I think he got Alexei involved. Which means Giovanni Romano is involved. Milo Hutch isn't going anywhere." He leaned down and kissed me softly. "Now. I have the perfect cure for claustrophobia." Curious, I followed him to a motorcycle. He climbed on and held out a hand for me. "Come on, honey. Let's ride."

Chapter Six
Eagle

Yeah, I should have put a helmet on her, but I knew how she felt. Sometimes, when the memories and nightmares got to be too much, I needed the wind in my hair and the sun on my face too. It was close to midnight now, the night hot and humid. Perfect for riding. At least for me.

Nyla wrapped her arms around my waist and we took off. For the longest time, she didn't move. Then I felt her face against my back and she rubbed against me like a cat. I patted her hands with one of mine and continued on. I had a place in mind. It was away from the main compound of the club, but we owned it. A swimming hole off a stream that had deep, cold water. It would feel good in the heat of the night.

I pulled the bike next to the wooden landing the club had made with a ladder making for ease of getting in and out of the water. "Can you swim?" I asked her once I'd shut the bike off.

"No," she said softly. "But I've always loved the water. Are we going swimming?"

"Thought we might. It's cold and deep. You can hang on to me and I'll keep you safe."

She smiled up at me. "I know. Thank you, Eagle. For... you know." She heaved a sigh. "For everything."

I cupped her face between my hands and leaned in to kiss her. "You're very welcome. Now. Let's get naked."

She barked out a laugh. When I started stripping, though, she followed suit without hesitation. I jumped in, the cold water enough to take my breath. It was refreshing and welcomed me like an old friend.

"Come on, baby. Don't think about it. Just jump

in."

"But you said it was cold." I could see her lithe body in the silvery moonlight. Her breasts were a perfect handful and stood high and proud. The rest of her was layered with fine muscle. She grabbed the top of the ladder for balance and dipped her foot in the water before jerking it back out again. "Are you kidding me? It's like ice water!"

I couldn't help but laugh. "Come on. A little cold water never hurt anyone."

"You're crazy."

"Never said I wasn't. Either come on in, or I'm coming after you."

"Fine," she muttered. Taking a deep breath, she leapt off the landing right into my arms. Naturally, we both went under for a second, but she was all right. "Fuck! Christ! It's fucking *cold*!"

"So? Just means we'll have to stick close to keep warm."

"You better not let me go, Owen Asher! You do and I will not be pleased."

"Never, baby. Not in a million years." Kissing her was a gnawing need inside me. There was no way to deny myself, and I didn't try.

Nyla moaned into the kiss and wrapped her arms around my neck, meeting my tongue as I dipped it inside her mouth. My cock, though protesting the cold water, stirred to life almost immediately. I wedged it between our bodies and thrust, trying to get friction for both of us.

Her legs wrapped around my waist and she shifted a little to the left. When she got herself aligned just right, her breath caught and she let her head fall back on her shoulders.

"So good…" Her whispered confession delighted

me.

"Yeah, it is, baby. There's more where that came from. So Goddamned much more."

I cupped one of her breasts in my palm, squeezing gently and finding the nipple with my fingers. I tugged at it before squeezing her breast again. Then I lifted her enough to be able to reach her nipple with my lips. She sucked in a breath before letting loose a scream.

At first I thought I might have hurt her. I didn't think I'd been too rough, but it was sometimes hard to know. The battle earlier, the fear and rage, the death awaiting the men in the barn who'd hurt our women, all of it had me riding the edge of my control. Though, I had to admit, having Nyla wrap her slender arms around me while we rode had soothed me in ways I hadn't expected or understood. I needed to fuck her, but the beast inside me wasn't there like it usually was after this kind of thing.

"Do it again! Do it again!" She thrust her tits at me, her fingers finding my hair and fisting there and pulling me against her chest.

I grunted as I latched onto her nipple again. This time, I pulled strongly, stretching the bit of flesh until it sprang free from my mouth with a little pop. She immediately offered me the other breast which I gladly took.

Her keening cries filled the air along with the song of night bugs and frogs. A gentle breeze blew over our chilled skin and I couldn't tell if her trembling was from cold or desire. I knew I barely noticed the cold. All I registered was how wonderful Nyla's body felt against me and how delicious she tasted.

"I need you, Eagle. Please." She gasped, reaching between us to grasp my cock, positioning it at her entrance.

"Ahh!" I cried when I sank into her warm heat. The temperature difference was almost more than I could take without coming immediately. I bit my cheek to hold on, determined I was not coming before her. Never!

"Take what you need, baby. Talk to me."

"You feel so good inside me. Never felt this."

"Good. I'll always take care of you, baby. Fuckin' always!"

The water sloshed around us and several times I almost went under. Honestly, I could have cared less if I had. As long as she didn't and was able to get the pleasure she needed. Learning she'd never orgasmed before our first time had been difficult to process. How could anyone have sex with this woman and not want to see her come was beyond me. That stopped with me. If there was any way possible, she'd never leave my arms unsatisfied.

"Yes!" She cried out, her body shuddering around me. Her pussy squeezed and milked my cock. "I'm coming! Oh, God!"

"That's it, baby. Make me come with you."

She screamed, her pussy clamping down impossibly tighter around me. That was it for me. I shot my cum deep inside her, tightening my arms around her and holding her close as I shuddered and groaned out my release.

Our breathing was ragged in the night. Her body was limp, and I wasn't far from it. Had we not been over our heads in the water, I'd have collapsed. As it was, I had to fight to keep us above the water. I couldn't ever remember being happier.

"Wow." Nyla robbed her face against mine like a contented cat. She found my mouth with hers and gave me a lingering kiss.

"No shit," I chuckled. "Life with you's gonna be a delight."

"You promise it's OK if I stay? I don't want anyone to get hurt."

"Honey, I told you. We got this taken care of. Even if we didn't, none of this is your fault. I hate that you had to go through this, but I'm glad you were here where you're safe. You've got me and every other man in Iron Tzars here to protect you."

"Too bad you're unable to do that." The voice was male and filled with malicious amusement.

Nyla sucked in a breath. "Milo." Her voice was barely above a whisper.

"Nyla, my dear. You've been very naughty."

"You're a monster," I snapped. "Leave us alone!"

"Now, now. No need to continue your role. I have what I need from this club." He held out his hand like he fully expected Nyla to take it. "Come."

"You've lost your mind," she bit out. "Get away!"

"Now, that's not nice." He reached behind him and pulled a gun from behind his back, chambering a round before pointing it at us.

I shoved Nyla behind me, keeping a firm hold on her with one arm, clamping her to my back. "You won't harm her," I said softly.

"Oh, I have no intention of harming her. She makes me money."

Milo Hutch pulled the trigger. I jerked back as pain exploded through my shoulder. Nyla screamed and I lost my grip on her. Milo cackled like a maniac as another shot rang out. This time, pain exploded through my temple and my world went black.

* * *

Nyla

I screamed. And screamed.

And screamed.

"Little Nyla," Milo said, *tsking*. "I'd have thought you'd know by now no one escapes me. You're mine, little girl. You'll always be mine."

"NO!"

I struggled to stay above the water. Eagle was face down in a deadman's float. Grief burned in my gut as I reached for him to try and turn him over in case he was still alive. Blood streamed from his temple. Could he survive a shot to the head?

"Get out of the water, bitch." Milo's tone had changed. Now he sounded as angry as I ever heard him. "It's time to go."

"What did you mean when you said you had what you needed from this club?"

He shrugged. "I was trying to get him away from you so I had a clear shot. I thought it might be easier if he thought you'd betrayed him. While I have no problem with killing you, I wasn't kidding when I said you make me money. To hear them talk, you have magic in that pretty pussy of yours. I hadn't thought to try it out myself, but I think I'll be remedying that now." He gave a sinister laugh.

I was struggling to keep my head above water. Eagle still hadn't moved though he was now face up in the water. Blood poured from his head wound and I had no idea how badly he was hurt or if it was already too late to save him.

"Come to me, Nyla! Come to me and I might let you live!" He roared his demand, sounding like he was no longer sane.

"Go fuck yourself," I hissed. If I was going to die,

it would be on my own terms, and it would be with Eagle.

"When I pull you out of that water, little girl, I will give you to the worst sort of men you could ever imagine! You'll be torn apart and I'll laugh as I drink your blood!"

"You're crazy!" I was sobbing now. Eagle wasn't moving. "I'll die before I let you have me again!"

"No, you won't. You'll come with me because, like all women, you crave life. You're too soft to actually take your own life. Not when you have the chance of living."

I didn't want to die. But a future in the hands of a sadistic madman, a future without even a glimmer of hope Eagle would find me... wasn't a future I wanted. Owen Asher was the first man I'd ever known who treated me with decency. His club had as well, but Eagle was the first. He was the only man I'd ever willingly given myself to and I'd done it eagerly. Did I love him? As much as I knew what love was, I supposed I did. If our positions were reversed, he'd guard my body with his last breath and that's what I intended to do with him.

A shot rang out in the night. Milo screamed in pain. Blood sprayed from his body in the night breeze and he fell forward onto the landing. I screamed as I went under. Blindly, I reached for Eagle but he'd floated away from me.

"Help!" I struggled to stay afloat, only surfacing long enough to suck in a breath and scream one single word. The more I fought, the harder it was to keep my head above water.

Someone grabbed my arm and I screamed, lashing out even as I went under again. A strong arm went around my chest and lifted me to the surface.

"Take a breath, Nyla!" The command was stern, the voice familiar.

"Eagle!"

"We got him. Stitches is with him. He's breathing."

"What?"

"Stop fighting me!"

I turned my head to see Cyrus behind me, taking us to the shore a short distance from the landing. Sure enough, Eagle sat in the grass while Stitches looked at his head. He didn't look like he knew where he was, but the second he spotted me, he yelled.

"Nyla!"

"Eagle!" I struggled, needing to reach him more than I needed to breathe.

"Easy girl! You're gonna drown us both!" Cyrus kept moving with sure strokes. How he managed to drag me along with one arm and swim with the other I'll never know.

The second my feet touched the muddy bottom, I stumbled to the grassy bank and crawled on my hands and knees the few feet to Eagle. Stitches had ahold of him, holding him back from coming after me. I flung myself into his arms and completely lost my mind, crying and grieving with all the subtlety of a raging bull.

"I've got you, baby. You're safe." He was trying to comfort me when I could feel him trembling as he held me.

"Me? You were shot in the head!"

"He grazed me. Knocked me silly, but you saved me by turning me face up in the water."

"I thought he'd killed you!"

"I'm all right, honey. I swear, I'm all right."

"I want to go home," I whimpered.

"We need to get you to the hospital, Eagle," Stitches insisted. "I'm pretty sure you're good, but I'd rather get a CT to make sure you don't have a skull fracture."

"Yes," I whimpered. "Do that. I'll go with you."

"Baby, you're naked and wet. Let the guys take you home, and I promise I'll be right behind you."

"No! I'm not letting you out of my sight!"

"Fuck," Stitches muttered.

"What the hell happened?" Eagle demanded. "I thought Milo was locked up!"

"Not sure," Cyrus said as he got out of the water. "If Wylde hadn't been keeping an eye on him we'd never have known he'd gotten out."

"He said he locked him in a hole and threw away the fuckin' hole! What the fuck?" Eagle was livid. Anyone could hear it in his voice.

"Yeah," Stitches muttered. "That's not going away any time soon."

"Not if I can help it." Cyrus sounded more irritated than angry, but then he wasn't like the other men at Iron Tzars. I couldn't process that now.

"I thought I'd lost you." My strangled whisper was so soft I wasn't sure if he heard me. I was talking more to myself than Eagle, though. I burrowed as close to him as I could, needing to reassure myself he was really alive.

"You didn't, baby. I'm right here. Bit worse for wear, but I'm still with you."

"How did he even find us?"

"Don't know. But we'll find out."

"Is he dead?"

"He will be." Cyrus looked toward the landing and I followed his gaze. Two men from the club had him on his chest, tying his hands behind his back and his feet together. They'd gagged him, but Milo still struggled to get away.

"They shot him in the belly," Stitches said. "Not sure if he'll make it to the barn with the others, but either way he won't be alive long."

"Too fuckin' bad," Eagle snapped. "I'd like to take him apart slowly. Over fuckin' days. Months!"

"How about we get you to the hospital? I'll get a buddy of mine to do the CT off the books. We'll get you back to the clubhouse in half an hour if all is well."

Thank God, Eagle didn't have a skull fracture. True to his word, Stitches got us home in record time. Eagle refused help walking inside the clubhouse to his room, but we managed.

Stitches got him cleaned up and most of the blood out of his hair at the hospital, so when we finally stumbled into his room, he collapsed on the bed with a groan.

"Fuuuuuck."

"Same."

I undressed us both before crawling under the covers. Eagle reached for me and pulled me against him so my head lay on his chest, his fingers sifting gently through my hair. Thank God I'd been able to shower at the hospital as well because I didn't want my hair to smell like pond water.

"Of all the things that happened tonight, you're worried about your hair smelling like pond water?" I thought he sounded amused, but I was just too Goddamned tired and mentally exhausted to chastise him.

"Did I say that out loud?"

"Yeah, honey." This time he actually chuckled. "You did."

We lay there for a long time. I was so tired I

could barely keep my eyes open, but my mind was whirling a million miles a minute.

"We should do something for Rose when she gets home. I don't know what, but something to give her some closure. I don't want her to feel alone or like she has to keep it all inside."

"We will. We'll all help Atlas take care of her."

"Do we know how Milo found us?" I had to know. I also needed to know he wasn't just captured but that he was dead.

"Wylde admitted he underestimated Milo. Said he had several of the guards in lock up on his payroll and he overlooked it. They got him out through the back door. The system thinks he's still locked up, so no one will even know he's dead until Wylde unlocks his file or whatever. Even the guards who let him loose won't know what happened. Not that they'd care. Their job was to get him out of jail. Not to track him afterward."

"When will he die?" I had to know.

"Probably not long, if Stitches is correct. He'll keep Milo alive for a while, but Sting will likely let him die sooner rather than later. Much as we want him to suffer for what he did to all of us, he knows everyone is safer with him dead. Never say his name outside these walls, Nyla. Not for any reason. As far as anyone can prove, we never knew the bastard."

"What about the men who sent the drone?"

"They're being taken care of. My guess is Atlas will make them all die extra hard for what they did to Rose. Brick too."

Again we lay in silence. Then Eagle asked me a question. "You told us the day you got here Milo was with a man he called Dom. That this man was there when Milo was having a young girl undress."

"Yeah."

"Did you ever hear mention of a club called Grim Road?"

I thought for a moment, trying to remember. "That name is familiar, but I'm just not sure."

"I did a run with them right before you came to me. Grim Road takes down human traffickers. Dom isn't an unusual name, but you also mentioned a guy named Claw. Both of them are members of Grim Road. If they were there, if they were working out a deal with Milo, then whatever Milo was doing was some sick shit. Grim Road only goes after the worst of the worst because they never leave anyone alive." He took a breath. "I have... issues. When I was a medic in the service, I saw some pretty horrific things, but all that is nothing compared to the shit I've seen tagging along with Grim Road. I'm talking genocide and things so deviant it makes my skin crawl to think about them. I sometimes have nightmares and I lash out."

"If you're trying to tell me you might hurt me, I won't believe it."

"I admit, since meeting you, my mind has been so obsessed with you I seemed to have shaken off the last of the nightmares. I just want you to be aware."

"I'll keep it in mind."

I was just about to doze off when he murmured into my hair. "I love you, Nyla. I'll always love you."

"I love you too."

With those words, something inside me settled. I took a deep breath, let it out...

And slept.

* * *

Weeks later...
Eagle

"Owen... Eagle!"

I woke with a start, gasping. Sweat soaking my body. I leaned up, resting on my elbows while Nyla gently stroked my chest.

"Fuuuuck..." I collapsed back onto the bed, breathing like I'd run a marathon. I was surprised at the ease with which I woke. I hadn't had the urge once to fight. Only to follow the sweet voice calling my name. "Sorry I woke you, baby."

"Are you all right? Do you want to talk about it?"

"Not much to talk about. Literally. I have nightmares and usually wake up fighting. They usually surface after violent runs or when I have to participate in the barn."

She hadn't asked about the men we'd had in the barn, but I knew she was curious. Nyla was surprisingly gentle when it came to club business. Even stuff that involved her or that she was affected by. Like the bastards we'd taken apart in the barn.

We'd tortured them. Atlas especially. Milo had lasted longer than I'd thought Sting would allow, but Atlas had insisted. And he'd taken revenge in unspeakable ways. Sting had sent me back to Nyla when I'd shown up to finish it. The other man hadn't wanted me participating in the first place because I still had problems from the run with Grim Road.

"Then you won't be participating in any barn activities for a while. Will you." It wasn't a question.

I sighed. "Honey..."

"I don't ask you anything about club business or what's going on with Milo and the others. I never will. That's something I learned a long time ago. Don't ask. I'm assuming it's the same with this club?"

"Not with you. Or any of the old ladies. We may

keep some things from you, but only if we think you'd be in danger. Anything you want to know I'll tell you because this is your life and you have a right to know." Which brought up another issue I needed to tell her about. "Speaking of, have you talked to the other women about getting your tattoo?"

"I have. I know this is a for-life arrangement, and I'm on board. They also said their men got tattoos as well. Is that something you'll do?"

"I will." I got up to wash off the sweat. Nyla followed me and climbed in the shower behind me.

She wrapped her arms around me, pressing the side of her face to my back. "Thank you, Eagle. Thanks for saving me."

"Honey, you saved me too. Just in a different way. Since you've been with me, the nightmares have eased. You... soothe me. Even my brothers have commented on it."

"So have the club whores," she muttered.

"What?"

"Oh, nothing." I turned to find her smiling brightly at me.

I narrowed my gaze at her. "Has something happened I need to know about?"

"Not much." She shrugged. "I might have bitch-slapped someone. But she was looking at your ass and said she was making a play for you since you'd finally calmed down. Far as I was concerned, she deserved it. I don't share."

The chuckle that bubbled up inside me broke free before I could stop it. Hell, I wouldn't have stopped it if I'd been able to. "Little bit bloodthirsty, are you?"

"Damned straight! I just found you. I'm not giving you up easily. When you said this was forever, I took it to heart. I don't share and I don't expect you to either. Not sure how everyone else does it, but that's how we're doing it."

"God, I love it when you get all bossy." I quirked a smile at her. "Makes me hard."

A slow, satisfied expression graced her features. "Good."

Then she proceeded so show me why it was a good thing.

I love my life…

Cyrus (Iron Tzars MC 8)
A Bones MC Romance
Marteeka Karland

Odette -- My life has gone down the toilet. I accidentally got myself involved with a married man and had an... accident. Don't get me wrong, I didn't love the cheating bastard, but I hate that I got played. Naturally I did what any self-respecting eighteen year old would do. I went to a karaoke bar and got wasted. Not my finest moment. So, when I land in the arms of a man I've fantasized over for the past two years, I'm not even surprised. My luck is just that bad.

Cyrus -- The first time I met Odette she was only sixteen and already more trouble than I knew what to do with. She'd been about to make a mistake with a prospect from her brother's club when I intervened. The next time I see her, two years later, she's singing like an angel, drunk off her ass. I have to get her out of that bar. Taking her home with me to our club doctor feels like the right thing to do. Deciding she's mine to care for and protect might make me a possessive bastard, but I don't like the word *no* so I'm not giving her the chance to object.

Chapter One

Cyrus

"I can't understand why this amuses you." I was sitting with Blaze and Wylde in a bar a couple towns over from Evansville. It was karaoke night. Which was basically grown men and women, drunk off their ass, singing off-key and off-beat. Some people laughed, others whooped and clapped. I was at a complete loss as to what to do. Though, I now understood why people drank. If I did, I'd be drinking now. Heavily.

"It's laughing with each other and thinking how bad that person was and that you can do better. Only to get up on stage and do just as bad or worse." Wylde grinned at me as he explained. The bastard always loved explaining social nuances he knew I'd never get otherwise. It pissed me off sometimes because I knew he was having fun at my expense, but I was oddly grateful for the explanation. Not that I'd ever admit that. "Think of it as male bonding with both men and women."

"Seems like it's grown adults making fools of themselves." I winced as someone made a particularly horrible noise from the stage.

"Exactly!" Wylde was excited, almost like a kid. This was one of his favorite things to do. He always wrangled someone to go with him so he could drink. Of all the men in Iron Tzars, Wylde puzzled me the most. He was ruthless when it came to hunting people he considered "bad guys," but otherwise obeyed the law to the letter. I didn't understand him. "But that's not why we're here."

I pinched the bridge of my nose with my thumb and finger. I felt a nauseating headache coming on. "Then why the fuck *are* we here?"

"Just wait. Trust me when I tell you it will be worth the wait." Wylde actually looked gleeful. What the fuck was he up to?

"He's been talking about this for two weeks, Cyrus." Blaze tossed back a couple peanuts from the bucket on our table. "I'm actually anxious to find out what all the fuss is over." Blaze signaled our server that he and Wylde needed more beer. I took another cup of coffee.

"Well, he's got ten more minutes, then I'm outta here. You guys can either come with me or find your own Goddamned way home."

"I'd almost forgotten what an asshole you are, Cyrus." Wylde didn't look mad. Strangely, he looked amused.

"Never claimed to be anything but."

Wylde just grinned and took another pull from his beer. "You, my friend, are getting ready to be knocked on your ass."

With a roll of my eyes, I took a sip of the coffee in front of me. How was this even my life right now? Wylde had coerced me and Blaze into coming with him. Blaze was having a blast. Wylde too, obviously. This was a special kind of hell for me. I didn't deal with crowds on the best of days, and drunken, singing crowds made me want to run from the room screaming with my hands over my ears.

Wylde actually looked like a kid who'd been let loose in a candy store with a hundred dollars. He was practically rubbing his hands together with glee.

"I've got a bad feeling about this," Blaze said with a chuckle.

"Trust me." Wylde grinned at the other man. "You're gonna be glad you came." Then he burst out laughing.

"You're drunk." I ground my teeth. This was yet another reason I hated coming to shit like this. The guys knew I didn't drink and always wanted me to go because I was guaranteed to be the designated driver.

"Nah. Not this time. I'm just buzzed enough to really look forward to seeing your reaction to my little surprise."

I turned to Blaze. "He knows I hate surprises."

"Yep." Though Blaze knew how fine the control on my temper was most days, he looked like he was loving the anticipation as much as Wylde was.

"I may end up killin' you both."

Blaze shrugged. "Some things are just worth it."

Granted, I had trouble reading people. I never got other people's emotions. Hell, I had trouble with my own emotions. Expressing myself was difficult on the best of days. I'd given up trying to figure out everyone else a long fucking time ago. Usually, Wylde was with me to translate when I didn't get something so whatever he knew was getting ready to happen would likely knock me on my ass. As far as people went, Wylde and Blaze were probably the only two who understood me. They just used that knowledge to torment me sometimes. Said it was their way of showing they cared.

Whatever.

I stood and stalked to the bar as whichever poor bastard on stage tried to hit a high note in *Bohemian Rhapsody*. So help me God, if I made it out of this with my sanity intact, I was gonna kill Wylde tomorrow. I wanted him to be completely sober so he could fully appreciate the pain he was going to experience before he begged me for death.

Another cup of black coffee was set in front of me, and the bartender gave me a slight nod as he winced at the same drunk singer on stage. I'd never fully appreciated the phrase "infernal caterwauling" before until tonight.

The song ended and there was a rousing round of applause. Probably because the song was over. "Thank fucking God," I muttered into my cup as I took a sip. What I wouldn't give to be called away on a mission. Or even to weapons testing for Shadow Demons. Mindless target practice sounded like heaven.

Then the next song started and I wanted to bang my head against the bar. Of course, that was before the singer opened her mouth to belt out the lyrics to a raucous country and rock hybrid.

She was fucking *good*, her voice a strong, sultry contralto with the perfect amount of rasp. I perked up, setting down my coffee and straining to see the small figure on stage. Me and everyone else. The bar, which had been moderately sedate, seemed to come alive and spark with excitement the second the music started.

The woman on stage engaged the crowd with her presence alone. Just looking at her, one would never be able to tell she had such a big voice. Not only that, but her charisma was off the fucking charts. She had every fucking horny-ass motherfucker in the fucking bar moving toward her. Some were whooping and hollering, singing the song with her like it was some rock anthem at a stadium concert. Some swung women around on the dance floor, but every single one of them was homing in on her. And the little witch looked disturbingly familiar.

As she danced on stage and flirted with the audience, I became aware I'd left the bar and was moving toward her myself. I'd love to say I was caught up in the moment, in the music and the spontaneity of it all. I'd love to say that. But the fact was, it was the woman. Her beauty and sexuality. Her passion for life and people. And I knew the little witch! How the fuck had she ended up here?

Odette Muse was trouble with a capital *T-R-O-U-B-L-E*. She was also the much younger half-sister of a man I knew when we were in the Air Force together. Last I heard, he still lived in Palm Beach, Florida, and rode with a club called Salvation's Bane. I'd met Odette there where she was trying to sneak into the compound with a prospect she was way too good for. At sixteen she'd been a free spirit. In love with life and all the pleasures of the flesh, so to speak.

That had only been two years ago, but it was a memory that was clear as fucking crystal. I'd stopped her from fucking that prospect by dragging her back to her brother, but I had no doubt she'd found someone else. Hopefully a man more worthy of her beauty and passion. As well as closer to her own fucking age. Though now, at eighteen, I suppose it didn't matter as much.

I clenched my fists as I made my way toward the stage like I was in a trance. Emotions were elusive for me. Things better left in a sealed box inside my mind. Not today. Rage like nothing I'd ever experienced poured through me like molten lava. Hot and viscous. It clung to my insides and seared me from the inside out as I watched other men watching her. Touching her when she danced near them as she sang fucking karaoke. I wasn't good with emotions. Mine or anyone else's. So this punch to the gut was as unwelcome as it was unexpected.

Odette was better than this. She should sing her own songs. Be in a famous band. Anything other than the main entertainment at fucking karaoke night in a backwoods bar. I was torn between jerking her off the stage and taking her out back to spank her delectable ass, or killing any motherfucker who touched her. Maybe I'd do both.

I'd just reached the stage when the song ended. She stood there with a huge smile on her face, holding a microphone while she waved at the cheering crowd. Odette jumped straight up, throwing her arms in the air in joy, laughing like she didn't have a care in the world. What the fuck was she doing here? And why wouldn't Blade give us a heads-up if he knew his sister was coming this way?

She stumbled sideways and nearly fell on her ass. Thank God I was there to catch her, or she'd have broken her fool neck falling from the stage. Like she hadn't just fallen off the stage right into a strange man's arms, Odette laughed and threw her arms around my neck. I could smell the alcohol on her the second she dropped into my arms but also her own faint scent of honeysuckle. That scent had haunted me ever since the first day I met Odette.

The little nymph buried her face in my neck and inhaled. "Ain't smelled a man like you since I tried to nail me a biker." God, that sultry voice! The woman had me hard as a fucking rock with just her fucking voice. And her scent. And the softness of her skin. The crowd roared and the people next to us pawed at her. She seemed oblivious as she nuzzled her face against my skin. "So delicious..."

"Snap out of it, Odette!" I growled at her. No clue if she heard me or not, but I doubted she did. Even if it wasn't so loud I couldn't hear myself think in there, especially once another song started up and the next singer belted out her song as loud as Odette had, I was pretty sure Odette was completely wasted. Anything I said or did until she sobered up would be a waste of time and breath.

I moved to the front of the bar and the exit, needing to get her out of there so I could at least make sure she was OK. Blaze and Wylde fell in step beside me. Wylde was cracking up, Blaze grinned but shook his head. Whether it was at me or Wylde I had no idea but it had better have been Wylde. I wasn't in the mood.

"Bro, I wish like fuck you could've seen your face when you realized who was up on stage." Wylde was wheezing he was laughing so hard.

"Wylde, you might want to back off for a while," Blaze advised, clapping the younger man on the shoulder. "Don't think this is the time."

"Need a cage." My voice was rough with anger, and I nearly bared my teeth at Wylde. "Not your fuckin' mouth."

"Not to worry. I got Clutch bringing the Bronco. He can take your girl back to the compound." Thankfully, Blaze still had his head on straight. Though, like fuck Clutch was doing anything with my girl.

Except she wasn't my girl. I didn't say anything, but no one -- *no one* -- was touching Odette but me. That included my brothers. *Especially* my brothers. Because she had a thing for bikers. Probably all the men her brother hung around. Blade had never made it a secret he belonged to an MC. Even in the conservative area he lived in, he wore his colors loud and proud.

Sure enough, it wasn't but a couple seconds, I saw Clutch pull around the corner in the dark blue Bronco. He rolled down the window and grinned.

"Need a lift?" He flashed a friendly half smile when he rolled the window down.

"No," I snapped. "Get out."

Clutch's demeanor changed in an instant. "You lettin' me ride your bike? 'Cause I gotta tell you. I'm pretty fuckin' fond of this cage and I know how much you love that fuckin' Harley."

I did bare my teeth this time. "Get. Out."

"You're my brother, Cyrus. And I know you got issues but I'm the road captain in this outfit. Which means I fuckin' outrank you. And you don't get to fuckin' tell me what to do with the fuckin' cage."

"Long story, Clutch," Blaze offered. "Take his bike and I'll fill you in."

Somewhere in my mind, I knew there was a reason I should protest Blaze giving Clutch permission to ride my bike, but all I could focus on at the moment was Odette. She'd passed out in my arms soon after she started sniffing my neck. Now she was snoring softly, her lips against my skin. She was fine now, but how would she do on the ride home?

"Where's Stitches?" I wanted him to check her over before I put her to bed. Might be something other than alcohol and I needed to make sure.

Blaze opened the passenger door to the cage and I settled Odette in, reclining the seat back a bit so she had a better center of gravity. I didn't want her pitching forward or to the side as I drove.

"Think he had a shift tonight. Want me to have him come see you when he gets off?"

I met Blaze's gaze with what I was sure was a hostile one of my own. "No, dumbass. I want you to tell him I need his fuckin' ass at the fuckin' clinic. Now."

"Not sure it works that way, Cyrus." Blaze scrubbed the back of his neck. "How 'bout I tell him we're meetin' him at the hospital. He can tell you what you need to do then."

Wylde let out an angry squawk as Clutch practically tossed his drunk ass in the back seat. "Not a word outta you, Wylde. And don't fuckin' puke in my cage!" Clutch snarled. "You do, I'll take the cleanin' out in your hide."

"Ain't gonna puke." Wylde rested his head against the back of the seat.

"Yeah? The sweat on your brow and the way you're slurrin' your words say otherwise." Clutch went to the back and opened the tailgate. He rummaged around before shutting it and thrusting a barf bag in front of Wylde. "You puke in the fuckin' bag. Get me?"

"Sure thing. You don't gotta be so mean." His eyes were closed and he held the bag in his hand resting on his leg, but made no move to ready it for use.

Clutch ground his teeth and pointed at me. "You're responsible for that fuck."

"Nope. He got himself drunk. He's responsible for his own Goddamned self. Me being designated driver is the only reason I'm lettin' him in here now."

"How the fuck were you gonna be the DD without a fuckin' cage?"

I shrugged. "Wylde rode bitch. Always does. Blaze never drinks enough to not be safe on a bike. Besides, that's why we keep you on."

That wasn't true. He was road captain so he was in charge of any runs we did. It was a complicated process where he had to plan out routes that didn't intersect another club's territory without permission. He also kept the cages and bikes all in top working order. Anything happening while on a run was his responsibility. He was not required to be on call for anyone who got drunk and couldn't drive themselves back home. But he always was.

Clutch pointed at me. "You're on thin ice."

"You gonna ride my bike back to the clubhouse or not?" I was done here. I needed to get Stitches to check Odette over before I left her alone to sleep it off.

"Fine. Be warned you're on my shit list, you bastard."

"As long as I get what I want, I couldn't give a good Goddamn." I climbed in and took off before Clutch could change his mind.

I didn't wait for the notification from Blaze that Stitches was waiting on us. I moved it to the hospital and trusted my brother to be waiting when I got there.

"You're in so much trouble, little girl," I muttered even as I reached over to grab Odette's wrist to check her pulse.

"Ain't no little girl." Wylde mumbled from the back seat. I'd forgotten he was there.

"No. You're a little bitch," I snapped. "You knew she was here. Did you know how fucking' drunk she was, too?"

"Nah. Didn't see her tonight but she's been here every karaoke night for the last month. Never been drunk before."

"She know you saw her?"

"Nope."

I glanced in the rearview mirror at Wylde. He stuck his tongue out like he had a bad taste in his mouth, then scratched his balls and adjusted himself. Fucker. He was drunk off his ass. I was looking forward to making tomorrow a special kind of hell for the little fucker. Next thing I knew, he was snoring. It wasn't subtle.

The trip to the hospital where Stitches worked took me about fifteen minutes. During that time,

Wylde continued to snore. Every time he inhaled or exhaled, the noise got louder and louder. At least it seemed that way. I grabbed a bottle lid in the cup holder and threw it at Wylde. "Shut the fuck up, asshole! Wake up!"

"Wha'dja hit me for?" God. The bastard was whining. I hated whining.

"'Cause you're snoring like a motherfucker. I've slept under fuckin' train bridges that were quieter."

"Bastard…" He muttered his grievance before he was back to snoring. Odette didn't seem fazed by the noise at all. She slept peacefully in the seat next to me, a little half smile on her face like she was in pure bliss.

I had my fingers on her wrist at her pulse. I told myself I was ensuring she wasn't in danger, but the fact was, I loved the way her skin felt on mine. The steady beat of her pulse reassured me, but there was more to it than that. I needed Odette close and couldn't figure out why. Her brother was a badass as well as a very gifted pediatric oncologist. We'd saved each other's asses multiple times while on tour. I figured I owed him my loyalty because of all the shit we'd been through together. Maybe that was it.

Given that Blade hadn't called ahead and let us know his sister was in the area, he likely didn't know where she was. Which meant she was on her own. Which meant I had to take care of her until her brother was properly notified and had a plan in place to keep her safe. That was perfectly logical. That's why I needed to make sure she was all right. That her current state was self-induced alcohol intoxication instead of something more sinister. Like someone slipping something into her drink. That thought brought back the rage I'd fought against earlier. Which, again, was odd. Emotions never ruled me.

After parking the Bronco, I went around to Odette's side and picked her up. I shut Wylde in the vehicle with the fob safely in my pocket. As I walked across the parking lot with her, Odette wrapped her arms around my neck and snuggled in. Like she'd done before, she buried her nose in my neck and inhaled deeply before sighing happily and settling once again.

She weighed next to nothing. I'd tossed her over my shoulder and marched her straight to her brother the last time I'd seen her, but I was sure she was heavier back then. How much weight had she lost? And why? Surely, she wasn't on some kind of fucking diet. The woman had been too skinny two years ago.

"Girl, you need a keeper." I muttered to her as I got near the back entrance to the ER. I spotted Stitches leaning against the building, looking at his phone. The second he spotted us, he moved toward me.

"What happened?" His tone was no nonsense, something I appreciated after the fiasco with Wylde.

"Not sure. Probably just drunk, but anything is possible."

Stitches took out a pen light and checked her eyes. She cried out and flinched, turning her face into my shoulder to hide her eyes.

"S'op it!" Her words were slurred, but at least she was responsive.

"Smells like a brewery." Stitches sighed. "What makes you think she has something on board other than alcohol?"

"Nothing. Just covering all the bases. This is Blade's sister."

"Blade. Donovan Muse? With Salvation's Bane?"

"Yep. He and I were tight in the Air Force. Can't imagine he'd let her come all the way up here alone without givin' us a heads-up."

"Maybe he told Sting."

I shrugged. "Maybe. But Blade knows I'm here. He'd tell everyone in the Goddamned area he trusted to keep her out of trouble if he knew. That includes me."

Stitches scrubbed a hand over his face. "I suppose I can do a drug screen on her. Won't get specifics, but it can identify the main things."

"I just need to know that she's OK. If I need to get her treatment beyond supportive care."

Stitches nodded. "I can help you with that. Come on inside. Take her to my sleep room and I'll draw her blood. Got a lab tech who owes me a favor. I'll get him to run a drug screen on it. In the meantime, I can set her up with a banana bag. You can manage it at the clubhouse. If anything comes up in her drug test, I'll let you know what you need to do."

"Good."

I followed Stitches in the back and to a small room with a twin bed, a refrigerator, a TV, and a private bathroom. It was clean and looked like it hadn't been used this shift.

"Lay her down. I'll get some stuff to start an IV and draw her blood."

Ten minutes later, Stitches handed me a bag of bright yellow fluids with IV tubing in a separate package. He also gave her some Narcan just to be on the safe side, but it didn't seem to do anything. "Don't spike it until you get ready to use it. With the new dispensary, I had to practically give my left nut to get this under the table. Last thing I need is to have to get another one because you forgot to clamp off the tubing and it all leaked out before you got to use it."

"I may not have transitioned my medic license

into the civilian world, but I'm not stupid. I know how to manage IV fluids." I felt my temper spike again. This was insane. I hadn't felt anything like this since I was a kid. Before I'd learned how to bury any emotion I didn't understand deep inside me where it couldn't get out. "Ain't a dumbass."

"Sorry, man. Didn't mean to imply you were. Explaining myself is a force of habit. Fewer misunderstandings and accidents that way."

Blaze was waiting in the hall when I exited with Odette in my arms. She was sleeping peacefully.

"Thought you'd have more trouble with her." Blaze nodded toward the arm where she had an IV site at the bend of her elbow. "Didn't hear her cry out when Stitches stuck her."

"'Cause she didn't even fucking flinch." That worried me. The only time she'd reacted was when Stitches had checked her eyes. The rest of the time, she slept peacefully. "You sure I should take her back to the clubhouse, Stitches? What if she's been drugged with something that she needs to be monitored for?"

"Then I'll call and have you bring her back. I'm betting it's just the alcohol. She didn't have a reaction to the Narcan, so it's not anything with opiates involved. The best thing is for her to get those fluids and sleep it off. Main thing to watch for is vomiting. You don't want her on her back. Be best to have her on her side. That way she doesn't aspirate if she gets sick and she won't get smothered if she's too drunk to move the pillow away from her face if she's on her stomach."

I knew all this, of course. I didn't need anyone fucking telling me how to take care of a drunk. Looking down at her beautiful face, though, I felt a sliver of apprehension coil in my belly. This woman was in my care. She was the sister of a man I considered a close friend. Though every man in Iron Tzars MC was my brother, I didn't have many people I considered a friend. The compulsion to take care of Odette was too strong to ignore and that had to be because of my loyalty to Blade. Not because of Odette herself. She was nothing to me.

But as I continued to look at her, I grew more and more possessive of her. That feeling had nothing to do with my friend and everything to do with the woman in my arms. I shook myself. I had to get a grip on these feelings. This is why I hated dealing with emotions. There was no good reason for them. I didn't even know this girl! I'd met her exactly once and it hadn't been the best of meetings. In fact, I was pretty sure she hated me after I'd carried her like a sack of potatoes to her brother and ratted out her and the prospect she was with for sneaking into the Bane compound without getting permission from a patched member.

I took her back to the Bronco. Wylde was standing next to the cage, one hand braced on the back quarter panel while he bent double and heaved his guts up. There is nothing that smells worse than alcoholic vomit. If this was in Odette's future, I had no idea how I'd handle it. I told myself it was because the smell would be unbearable. In reality, I wasn't looking forward to seeing her as miserable as Wylde looked. Just the thought put a sharp pain in my chest, and I settled Odette closer to me, rubbing my cheek against her silky hair.

Then I jerked myself straight, letting her head fall back against my shoulder. What the fuck was this? Odette was drunk. An inconvenience at best. If she was miserable because she'd drank too much, it would serve as a reminder for her not to do this ever again! I should be looking forward to making tomorrow as miserable for her as I planned on doing to Wylde. But the thought made my chest hurt worse. There was no way I was going to be glad she was hurting and miserable. Why? Good Goddamned question.

Good Goddamned question.

Chapter Two
Odette

There was currently a freight train and a jackhammer storming and pounding their way through my head. My eyes felt like someone had thrown sand in them and my mouth tasted like my cat had shit in my mouth.

Lovely.

"Fuckin' bitch." I mumbled as I groaned and turned over. Thankfully, the room was dark. Woo-hoo for blackout curtains. Once on my back, the room spun horribly so I let my leg fall off the bed. Only it didn't touch the floor. So I groaned again as I scooted to the edge...

And promptly fell off the bed with a thud.

"Ohhhh..." I groaned, knowing I should get up. Instead, I lay on my back with my knees bent and didn't move.

"My, my, my. Someone had a rough night."

The voice was deep, gruff, and disturbingly familiar. "Fuck you." I threw out the insult with no real heat. It was reflex. Besides, who would have the audacity to approach me before I'd had my coffee? Whoever he was, he was just asking to get his balls handed to him.

"Need coffee."

"Yeah, that would probably help the headache. Got some Ibuprofen and Gatorade for you too. Want to feel better? You'll take them and go back to bed."

I squinted and looked up at the man standing over me. The room was dark so I couldn't see him, but I wasn't scared. Which was odd. I hated strange men getting too close to me. But this guy was different. At least, I thought he was. I had vague memories of him carrying me out of the bar.

"You smell good," I murmured to myself. Because he *had* smelled good. It was the strangest combination of outdoors musk, pine, and… gasoline? I remember thinking about the one time I was in the arms of a man who smelled like that. It had been two years ago, and the man was so off-limits it wasn't even funny. Which was why I'd been doing something I shouldn't have been doing. And why I hadn't minded so much getting caught.

"Yeah, you said that before." He knelt and lifted me into his arms. My stomach protested the movement and I whimpered, swallowing furiously and trying to keep the nausea at bay. "Bathroom," he said, carrying me. Which only made the nausea worse. Also, I *really* had to pee.

The guy seemed to understand my urgency because he made it to the bathroom fast. Just in time, too, because everything I'd ever eaten over my whole entire life and absorbed in the womb before I was born came up out of my stomach in a violent gush of foul-smelling, explosive puke. And I might have peed a little before I realized.

The toilet flushed and I startled. Oh. The good-smelling guy. Who knew just how much I'd debased myself. And had watched me puke my guts up. Lovely.

"Ohhhh…" I sat back on my ass, holding my head in my hands. I wished I could see him but my vision was blurry from tears and the needles stabbing through my eyeballs straight to my brain, making both hurt like a son of a bitch.

"Seem to be fond of that sound. I take it you're not used to this much alcohol?" God, his voice was yummy! I could listen to that raspy rumble every single day forever.

"Some woman's a lucky bitch and I hate her."

There was silence before he spoke again. This time, I didn't think he was talking to me. "Stitches back yet? Tell him I need him in my room. Now." There was a pause. "I don't give a flyin' fuck what the bastard's doin' right now, tell him to get the fuck up here!"

Wow. That sounded bad.

Stitches. That name was familiar. I should know who that was. Sounded like a road name, like my brother. His was Blade. I always thought it was because he was a doctor, but he said that wasn't it. And why was I thinking about my brother? I wanted to think about the man who'd carried me to the bathroom. Except, for some reason, I didn't want to think about him either. Or, more accurately, that he'd carried me to the bathroom and sat with me while I'd just brought up a comedic amount of puke…

I groaned. "This can*not* be my life right now." A washcloth appeared in front of me and I took it gratefully, wiping my face with the cool rag. "Thank you." I muttered. A glass of water appeared as well. He took the cloth and I took the glass, rinsing my mouth out before spitting it in the toilet and flushing. Then I gulped the rest of the contents down like I'd been a week in the desert with no water. My mouth felt like I had.

"Need a toothbrush."

"Got one ready." I shivered. That voice could melt panties across four counties. Scratch that. Across forty or fifty states. "Come on, lil' bit."

I froze. I'd heard that nickname only once in my life. Two years ago. "No." I shook my head, then groaned as both pain and dizziness assailed me. "God…"

"Pretty sure God had little to do with it. Stand up and brush your teeth. Stitches will be here in a minute."

I tried to get up, but my legs didn't seem to work. Neither did my balance. When I fell back on my ass, gentle hands lifted me into strong arms and the next thing I knew I was standing in front of the vanity at the sink.

"Open your eyes," he said. "Dizziness'll be worse if you keep them closed."

"Don't wanna open my eyes," I pouted.

"Afraid the real world will come crashing down around you?" His arm was solidly around my waist, holding me upright. My knees felt like Jell-O and the room was spinning so violently with me upright, I was pretty sure I was going to hurl again.

"Something like that." My voice was more of a whimper than anything else. It shamed me, given I was pretty sure I knew who this man was, but I was too sick and hung over to give it much thought. Which was kind of my motto. Never worry today about something you can put off until tomorrow.

"Open." His voice was commanding but gentle. In my weakened state, I had no choice but to obey that tone of voice coming from this guy. Who I was pretty sure I knew.

Taking a breath, I did as he commanded… and came face-to-face with the man who'd haunted my dreams for two fucking years.

"Why did it have to be you?" I looked into those dark eyes I'd seen every single time I closed my eyes, refusing to look anywhere else. Unable to look anywhere else. He mesmerized me the same now as he did two years ago.

"It had to be someone. You'd rather it had been

your brother?" He raised an imperious eyebrow at me.

"Ain't like he won't be here in less than twenty-four hours once you tell him. Besides, he's my brother. Not a man."

Cyrus actually barked out a laugh. "Can't wait to tell him that. How exactly would you classify him if not a man?"

"My brother."

Any humor in his eyes died in that instant. He knew what I meant, and he wasn't happy about the implication.

"Don't even think about it, Odette. I'm not the man for you."

"Nope. You're not." I straightened and pushed back against him. To my surprise, he didn't immediately let go. Instead, his grip around my waist tightened.

"Let me go."

"Not until we get a few things straight."

"Look, I'm gonna puke again."

He gave me a hard look and shook his head slightly. "Stitches is coming back to check on you. You're still dehydrated. How much'd you drink?"

"Too much," I snapped. "OK? I know I fucked up. I don't need you tattling on me to my big brother. Now get out."

I didn't really expect him to, but he did. Cyrus stepped back, holding my gaze in the mirror for a few more seconds before leaving the bathroom. Immediately, I wanted to call him back. Cyrus was my hero. My knight in shining armor. I'd never admit it to a soul, but the only reason I'd been with that prospect two years ago was to get inside the compound to get a closer look at Cyrus.

He'd been visiting my brother and I'd been

completely gobsmacked. He was aloof but larger than life. He strode into the compound like he owned the place. I'd been parked outside, waiting on my brother. Donovan -- Blade -- had refused to let me inside because I was under eighteen and because I honestly had no business there. I didn't want to hang with my older brother, and he wasn't letting me hang with the guys in the club. Or the girls. I could have probably conned him into letting me stay with the old ladies or some of the older girls, but it'd have been pushing it. Besides, Donovan knew me. He'd have known there was something up I didn't want to tell him.

There was a knock at the door, and I cringed. "Go away."

"Can't do that, Odette." That wasn't Cyrus's voice. "Not until I check on you."

I huffed out an exasperated sigh before stomping to the door and jerking it open. "There. See? I'm fine." When I would have slammed the door in his face, the bastard stuck his heavily booted foot in the way.

"Not happenin', little lady. Out with you."

"I need a shower."

"Not until I'm sure you ain't gonna fall on your ass and hurt yourself."

Yeah. I knew that tone. Heard it from my brother often enough. It was his doctor voice. The one that said, "This is for your own good," even when it was more about getting his way.

"Fine." I jerked the door all the way open and pushed past Stitches. Because, really, it couldn't be anyone else. "What do I have to do to convince you I can take a fucking shower on my own?"

"Watch your language." Stitches rummaged through his bag, not even looking at me as he scolded me.

"I'm not a naughty child. You don't get to tell me what I can or can't say."

"No. I'm the doctor who stole medicine from the hospital last night, putting my job and my career in jeopardy. All to help you."

"I didn't ask you to do that."

"No. You didn't. Do you know why?" Before I could answer he continued, never once looking up from his stash-o'-medical shit. "Because you were completely incapacitated. Did you do it on purpose?"

"Yup. Solidly. It might have been self-destructive behavior, but I did it. Why? Because I wanted to have a good time."

"Yeah?" Of course, he looked up this time. 'Cause, really, being an ass while not looking at me was totally off the table. He wanted to drive this home and, if I were honest, I didn't blame him. "Havin' a good time now?"

I stuck my chin up, not cowed in the least. "If you're implying I didn't know what was coming, you'd be wrong. I simply didn't care."

"All right. That's enough." Cyrus stepped closer to the bed where I sat waiting for Blade to do whatever he was going to do. "You may not care, Odette, but did you ever think there might be people in this world who did?"

"About how hungover I got?" I snorted. "No, Cyrus. I didn't. Why? Because it's no big deal! People get drunk all the time and manage to survive a long fucking while."

"Language." Both men spoke in unison, and I wanted to throw something at them.

"You know what? Fuck both of ya. I'm outta here." I stood to go, but Cyrus shoved me back down. Gently, but it was a shove nonetheless.

"Sit the fuck down. Stitches ain't done, and you and me gonna have a talk."

"You're not the boss of me." It slipped out before I could stop it. Yeah. That wasn't getting me anywhere in a big Goddamned hurry.

"That's pretty fuckin' evident, considering you're still sitting comfortably." Cyrus crossed his arms over his chest and looked down his nose at me with an angry glare, a look I'd seen from my brother on more than one occasion.

I narrowed my eyes at him. "Are you threatening to spank me?"

"I don't threaten, Odette. I'm simply stating a fact. Your brother is in the middle of something he can't get away from, though he wanted to do just that. Leave a child he's trying to help to come get your drunk ass and take you back to Florida because he loves you that much. He's supposed to call me today and let me know if he can safely leave. I told him not to, that I'd take responsibility for you, but he didn't want to do that. Probably because he knows I'll make you toe the line and he feels sorry for you."

"My brother should not feel sorry for me. I did this to myself and he knows it. I don't want or need his sympathy. Not for this."

"She's fine, Cyrus." Stitches interrupted a conversation I really didn't want him to hear, but I had completely forgotten about him listening. Which was just as humiliating as Cyrus seeing me like this. It was worse than that, actually. Cyrus had been the one to drag me out of that bar. I knew it because I remembered his scent. It was comforting even as it teased me with something I knew I could never have. "I brought a bag of fluids to give her. None of the vitamins it really should have, but I wasn't giving my right nut to go with my left one. Not for this. She'll feel better once it's in. Open it up and let it go as fast as gravity will let it."

He hooked a thin tube to the IV in my arm that I'd forgotten about. I was glad it was there because I hated needles.

Cyrus nodded, never taking his eyes from me. "Thanks, Stitches."

"I know you're waiting on the OK from Blade, but my advice is for you to put her over your knee and spank her ass until she can't sit for a fuckin' week." He shut his bag and gave me a hard look. "Your brother would be ashamed of the way you're acting."

OK, that hurt. I tried not to wince but wasn't sure I pulled it off. I knew I was being a little brat, but I felt awful. Only thing I wanted was to take a shower and sleep for a week.

Once Stitches was out the door, Cyrus knelt in front of me where I sat on the bed. "What's all this about?"

"Nothing." Childish? Yeah. But I wasn't ready to talk to him just yet. I'd come all this way for that very thing, but I never expected to find Cyrus like this.

"Uh-huh. Fine." He stood and hooked hung the IV bag from a pole Stitches had left. "Lie back and rest while this goes in. I'll bring you something light to eat and some more painkillers. Once that bag is empty and you've got more on your stomach than what I suspect is rum, I'll help you take a shower."

"In no reality are you helping me take a shower, Cyrus. I've been bathing on my own a very long time. I can manage. Even if I have to sit on the ledge to do it, I am not letting you help me." I was ignoring the fact that he knew me well enough to know it had been rum I was drinking. He likely knew about the Coke I drank with it too. If I dwelt on that little tidbit of information too long, I'd start fantasizing again.

He sighed and shook his head slightly. It was like he was having an internal argument with himself. And losing. "Sit back. I'll bring you some buttered toast and apple slices. You can nibble on that while those fluids go in. We'll talk about the rest later."

Cyrus left then, leaving me alone with my thoughts. He was right about one thing. My brother didn't need my dramatics. In his line of work, there was enough real-life drama to do anyone. I was ashamed of my behavior, but I didn't want to involve Donovan in this. I didn't even want to involve Cyrus, but he was the first person I thought to turn to. Why was anyone's guess. The only history we had was when he'd hauled me over his shoulder and marched me straight to my brother. It was probably the image I'd built of him in my mind over all this time. He was nothing to me. I was nothing to him. But in my little pea-brained mind, I'd latched on to him for some unknown reason and thought he could make everything better.

Well, he couldn't. And this was the only time I could ever allow myself to get this drunk. Shouldn't have done it this time and likely wouldn't have if I'd been thinking straight. I'd just wanted to chase away the pain. Unfortunately, everything wrong in my life was still there. Now it was time to deal with it. Alone. Which meant, I needed to get out of here and start planning for the future. A future that didn't include a grumpy, emotionally unavailable biker. No matter how much I wanted it to.

Chapter Three
Cyrus

"Stitches!" I jogged down the hall after the club doctor. He turned, waiting for me to catch up before we continued on together. "What did her blood test show?"

"Haven't reviewed them. Got a trauma in last night after you guys left that took up all my time, then you called me up here. I have them in my office. You can come with me if you want." Yeah.

"I need to know what I'm up against."

He shrugged. "You're up against an immature brat used to manipulating people to get her way."

I snorted. "I'm up against more than that. Being Blade's sister means I have to treat her with kid gloves."

"No, it doesn't," Stitches sneered. "That girl needs her ass busted. If Blade can't see that he's a dumb shit. And I know he's not a dumb shit. Do what you have to and keep her safe. That includes punishing her for putting herself in danger last night. What if you and the other guys hadn't been there? What would have happened to her?"

"I know. I still want the OK from Blade to take her in hand. He should get back to me in the next couple of hours." I hoped. I'd told him to take his time because Odette was safe and he had a very sick child he was helping. Not that Odette wasn't as important, but she was looked after. She was safe.

Stitches opened the door to his office and went around behind his desk. I sat on the couch opposite him, crossing one ankle over the opposite knee. He pulled out a couple pieces of paper from his briefcase and rested his forearms on the desk while he scanned over it.

He frowned as he read over first one page, then the second. Then the first. "Mother fuck..."

"Was she drugged?" I sat up straight, fury settling inside me like I'd never known. Emotions were hard on the best of days. I didn't understand them in others and had no idea what to do with my own. I preferred to be in my workshop, building and designing things for the stuff Argent Tech supplied us with. They'd give us a weapon or security measure and I... made it better. Only reason I didn't work at Argent was that asshole Giovanni Romano didn't like being upstaged. Well, that, and I didn't belong there. I belonged with Iron Tzars. My brothers.

"Nope. All alcohol. However, she has a positive pregnancy test." He looked up. "She or Blade say anything about her being pregnant?"

I felt like all the oxygen had been sucked out of the room. "She's... pregnant?"

"Yep. My lab tech friend ran a quantitative test to determine how elevated her HCG level was. By the math, she's maybe four or five weeks. Not far."

"So maybe she doesn't know."

"There is a very strong chance she doesn't know. But a home test would pick it up at this point." He sat back, rubbing his finger under his nose. It was a gesture I'd seen him do often when he was deep in thought. "Maybe she came up here for abortion care."

"There are other places she could have gone. Why here? At four to five weeks, she could still get it done in Florida."

"True..." Me and Stitches stared at each other a long moment. "You know her?"

"I dragged her back to her brother two years ago when I caught a prospect trying to sneak her in at

Salvation's Bane. She didn't have permission to be in the compound and was only sixteen at the time. The prospect in question was twenty-three. Said he didn't know she was underage, but Thorn didn't let that slide. Kicked the fucker out without a moment's hesitation."

"Good thing he wasn't here," Stitches muttered. "There any reason she might come to you?"

My gaze widened, then narrowed. "Me. Specifically me." Stitches nodded and I had to really think about that. "Ain't smelled a man like you since I tried to nail me a biker," I muttered, repeating the words she'd said when I picked her up from that bar last night.

"What?"

I brought my focus back to Stitches. "Just something Odette said last night when I carried her out of the bar."

Stitches whistled. "Was that a good thing or a bad one?"

"Well, she buried her face in my neck and called me delicious."

"Christ." Stitches grinned. Then chuckled. "Bro, you're so fucked."

"Bastard."

He shrugged. "Well, you wanted answers. I just read the paper and tell you what the numbers mean."

"Yeah, well, I still need answers." I stood. "She needs food in her stomach."

"And rest. And water. Hydrate her with something other than booze, will ya?"

"All over that."

"You gonna tell Blade?"

I paused. Was I? "Not sure. I'll have to think about that. I've already violated her privacy."

"Whoa there, brother." Stitches stood, raising the

lab test results once before tossing them to the desk. "She gave up that right when she chose to get blackout drunk and pass out in your arms. She scared the bejesus out of you and me both."

"I could just see having to call Blade and tell him his sister was brain-dead from alcohol poisoning."

"Same. So, any right she had to privacy went out the window with the alcohol she consumed."

I gave a crisp nod. "Fine. But I'm not telling him until I hear back from him. Ain't makin' a special call for this and I'm not telling him if he's eyeball deep in work. She's an adult. She can work this out herself. She has people here to help her through it, including me."

"Especially you." Any humor Stitches showed before now vanished. "Especially you, Cyrus. You get that, right?"

"I get she latched on to me for whatever reason. I never encouraged her to do so."

"At some point, you need to learn to play well with others."

"Why? All that does is invite someone else to force me into decisions I wouldn't otherwise make."

"It also puts someone in your life you care about. Who cares about you?"

I snorted. "All the more reason to avoid, as you say, playing with others. If you care about someone, they could leave you. Betray you." I clenched my teeth, pushing the memories back down where they couldn't overwhelm me.

"That can happen to anyone, Cyrus. Anyone can leave or die. Or betray you."

"Not here. Not at Tzars. We have a code --"

"That works for someone not betraying you, but not leaving. We all live dangerous lives. You saw what happened last month."

"Yeah. I did. Atlas lost a child and nearly his woman. Brick almost lost his woman." I snapped out my answer harsher than I should have, but that memory was a raw, ugly scar on my mind. They weren't my women or my child, but the whole experience had been... uncomfortable. Even now, I absently rubbed at my chest. We could have lost so much more that day than just our peace of mind. "I won't put myself in that kind of position."

Stitches gave me a knowing look but wisely, let it drop. "All right." He raised his hands in surrender. "But I think you're missing out on more than you realize."

"That's my problem, Stitches. Not yours."

With that, I stood and left. I needed to get Odette some food and make sure she was settled in. Then I'd turn her over to the old ladies. They'd see to it she had what she needed and was taken care of. I'd keep an eye on her, but from a distance. If she had some romantic hope I'd be the one to save her, she could think again. I didn't do old ladies. Or children. I couldn't. Either would make me vulnerable and I couldn't have that. Not again. *Never* again.

I snagged the food I'd promised Odette and stomped my way back to my room. Why I'd put her in there I had no fucking idea. I needed to get Roman to assign her another room. Her own. That created its own set of problems, but they wouldn't be *my* problems.

Opening the door, I stomped in... only to find Odette wasn't where I'd left her.

"Odette!" I barked out her name, irritation and something else filling me. "Get your ass out here!"

Nothing.

"Odette!"

I moved to the bathroom. The shower had been used recently, but there was no sign of her. I glanced around the room and spotted the trash can. She'd removed her IV and dumped it and the half-finished bag of fluids into it. Her clothes from last night were gone and the shorts I'd put her in tossed onto the vanity. I couldn't find my shirt. Further evidence she'd come here to see me.

"When I get my hands on you, little girl, I'm gonna beat your ass."

I pulled out my phone and shot a text to Wylde. If she had a phone on her he could trace it. He could also pull security footage and see if she'd already left the compound, and if so which way she went and if she was on foot.

Seconds later, Wylde facetimed me. "She left about fifteen minutes ago. Looks like she called an Uber. I hacked into her phone as well as the phone of the Uber driver. Looks like they're headed to *The Women's Hospital Deaconess*. She's gotten an appointment with an OB? What the fuck?"

"Send the address to my phone. Can you get all her paperwork filled out before she gets there?"

"Sure. Everything's electronic now."

"List me as her…" I winced. I couldn't believe I was saying this. "Husband."

"Duuuude…"

"Just do it! Then file the appropriate paperwork to make it a reality."

"Sting'll kill you, Cyrus. Literally. Then me, just for being involved."

"Only if she insists on a divorce. She won't."

"You're playing with fire, Cyrus. I like it." Fucker had the biggest shit-eating grin on his face in the history of the world. "What's your plan? Wait. You didn't knock her up, did you?"

"No, dumb shit. I didn't. But this is the only way to get her to let me help her."

"You know, you could just ask."

"And give her the chance of saying no? Not bloody likely."

"Well, if Sting doesn't kill you, I have a feeling Blade will. From what I hear, he didn't come by his name because he's a doctor. Since this is his kid sister, he's gonna have a helluva lot to say about this."

"Fully aware. It's a permanent situation."

"Still think you need to talk to Sting about this. He's gonna be pissed as hell."

"This ain't his choice," I snapped. "It's mine."

Wylde raised his eyebrows. "It's hers too, man."

"You leave that to me."

The bastard grinned brightly. "Knew you had a thing for her."

"I met her twice, Wylde. There's no way you can figure I have a thing for her."

"Bless your heart." He chuckled, shaking his head like he thought I was simple minded. "You forget I'm the motherfucking tech guy. You were more than a little preoccupied, so I did some snooping."

"Wylde. Imma throw you a beatin' like you ain't ever had."

"Don't blame me. Everyone else was worried too." The fucker continued to grin like an ape. "Your searches and browsing history tell me you're using this as an excuse to take that girl for your own. She feel the same?"

I shrugged. "She ran straight to me, didn't she?"

"I remember me being the one who dragged you to that bar last night. Not the other way around. You found her there. She didn't find you."

"How the fuck are you even upright? As drunk as you were last night, you should be holed up in a dark room, puking every other breath."

"What can I say? I'm resilient like that. Now. Your girl. I'll list you as her husband on her medical form, but I'm not actually filing a marriage certificate. Not until I get the go ahead from Sting."

"Wylde --"

"Sorry, brother." He grinned. "I value my life. And it ain't Sting I'm afraid of. Blade is a scary-ass motherfucker, and I want Sting as a buffer between me and him if I marry his baby sister off to a man in a club that doesn't allow divorce on pain of death." The meaning of his words was grave, but he still had that shit-eating grin on his face. "In the meantime, go get your girl. Find out what the fuck's goin' on."

"Not a word about this, Wylde. You do and I'll get Giovanni Romano to delete your *Fortnite* account."

Instantly, the man sobered, his face hardening like I'd just told him I'd kill his dog. "You do and I'll hurt you worse."

"Then keep your trap shut." I hung up on him before climbing on my bike and taking off. I had a runaway bride to track down. For some strange reason, imagining her reaction to having me listed on her medical form as husband had one corner of my lips raising.

Strange.

Chapter Four
Odette

"No paperwork?" That was odd. "But I've never been here before."

The lady behind the desk shrugged. "Apparently, they got enough from you when you scheduled your appointment." She smiled kindly. "Just have a seat. It won't be but a moment."

I shook my head, but wandered off to sit. I had two positive home pregnancy tests, but this would tell the whole story. I knew I needed to question the paperwork more thoroughly, but I was so nervous I couldn't think. If they said it was good, it was good. I'd given my information so quickly when I made the appointment, maybe they did have everything they needed.

As I sat in the corner, I jogged my leg and bit my thumbnail. What was I going to do if this was real? Surely it had been a test malfunction. A false reading. But on two different tests? From different manufacturers? When I'd gotten the first positive test, I'd bought another test of a different brand. Same result.

"Miss Muse?"

My head shot up, my gaze finding the nurse standing at the open door leading from the lobby to the exam rooms.

"That's me," I muttered, giving her a tentative smile.

She took me back to the nurses' station, weighed me, took my blood pressure, and had me pee in a cup. Once she put me in an exam room, she did a quick history and asked about my reason for seeing the doctor.

"I had a positive test," I mumbled. "Just wanted to make sure it was a false positive." I tried to smile, but didn't quite pull it off.

She smiled. "I need you to completely disrobe. Here's a gown and a drape. Just sit on the exam table and the doctor will be in shortly."

I did as she said, stripping quickly and putting on the gown. Unlike most hospital gowns, this one covered my back but left the front open. I pulled it together and wrapped the paper drape over my legs. Taking a deep, calming breath, I tried to empty my mind. If I were any more nervous, I'd probably cry. Might anyway.

The door opened without even a cursory knock and in walked...

"Cyrus?"

He shut the door and sat in the chair next to the doctor's work shelf. He leaned back, lacing his fingers over his belly and crossing his legs at the ankles.

"That's right. You got ten seconds to come clean."

I lifted my chin. "My life isn't your business."

"Yeah?" He lifted an eyebrow. "You ran, Odette. Straight to me. I want to know why."

I shrugged. "It's cooler up north. I don't like humidity."

"The truth, girl."

"I'm not a girl!" I raised my voice before realizing other people could likely hear us. "I'm an adult, Cyrus. Regardless of what you think, I didn't come here for you."

"That's two," he said casually. "I have a feeling you're not going to be sitting for a week." He gave me a slight grin, like this was amusing to him. Fucker. "Or longer."

"My life is none of your business."

"We'll see." The bastard smirked like he held all the cards. Well, I knew my rights. They wouldn't let him stay if I didn't want him here. He could take a hike because I wasn't going through this with him here.

"Why are you even here?"

"Like I said. You came to me."

There was a knock on the door. Before I could say anything, Cyrus answered. "She's ready."

An older man walked in the room, a smile on his face. He had platinum hair and a deep tan. "Good morning, Miss Muse. I'm Dr. Redding. The nurse tells me you had a positive pregnancy test?"

I winced, closing my eyes. I didn't dare to look over at Cyrus. Did he know?

"Yes." I wanted to elaborate, but what was the point? Besides, I didn't want to say anything more in front of Cyrus.

"Well, I think it's pretty conclusive. Your quantitative test would put you at four to five weeks. Does that fit the time frame?"

"What?" Quantitative test? "I mean, yeah. That's about right, but what do you mean by quantitative test?"

"Your blood test. It measures the amount of pregnancy hormone in your blood. I got it faxed over from the hospital lab a few minutes ago. Dr. Ewing had it sent over."

"Ewing?" Before I realized what I was doing, I glanced over at Cyrus. He just gave me a slight, superior smirk.

"She had a bit of a mishap last night. Doc gave her some fluids and took her blood to make sure nothing else was wrong."

"You know Dr. Ewing?"

"I do. We're Air Force buddies."

"Well then. Thank you for your service. As to this little mishap?" He raised an eyebrow. At Cyrus, the fucker.

"Let's just say she imbibed a little too much and got herself dehydrated. Dr. Ewing was just covering all the bases."

"Hmm." Dr Redding frowned at me. "It's not healthy to be doing that. Not while you're pregnant and certainly not in early pregnancy."

"I'm aware of that," I snapped.

"All evidence to the contrary." Cyrus never took his gaze from me. The frown on his face said he severely disapproved. He also didn't show any surprise at my little… surprise.

"Mr. Wolfe. Did you bring her to Dr. Ewing?"

"I did. Like I said. We're old buddies. I found her in a bad way and kept her safe."

"I have you listed as her husband. I take it you're the father?"

I gasped, staring at Cyrus. What the fuck?

"I am." He met and held my gaze, daring me to contradict him.

"Good! I'm not sure what happened, but I'm glad she has someone looking out for her."

"She does now."

The rest of the visit passed in a blur. The doctor did an ultrasound and confirmed the baby was where it was supposed to be inside me, gave me a prescription for some prenatal vitamins and nausea medicine, then set me up with another appointment in a month.

"Don't hesitate to let me know if you're excessively sick or have any problems whatsoever. If you can't reach me at the office, have Dr. Ewing contact me."

"Trust me," Cyrus said. "We will."

The doctor left and Cyrus moved to the door and stood in front of it. "Get dressed. I'll take you home."

For some reason, that hit me like a punch to the gut. Tears burned my eyes and my throat tightened up. "I don't... I don't have a home."

"Yeah, you do. I'll take you there. Get dressed."

I shook my head, but did as he instructed. I managed to get my underwear and shorts on but struggled with my bra. Cyrus was there, helping me straighten out the pullover sports bra before putting my T-shirt over my head. When I turned around, he settled his hands on my hips.

"You good?"

Was I? "I don't know." Tears I'd been holding back for a week overflowed and fell down my cheeks. Gazing into Cyrus's eyes, I'd never felt more vulnerable in my life.

"You held it together this long. Hold on a little longer. Can you do that? For me?"

I sniffed and wiped the tears from my face, nodding as I did. "I'm good. I won't embarrass you."

He growled and pulled me into his embrace, holding me tightly. "Never, Odette. You could never embarrass me. For any reason."

I trembled, struggling to keep myself together, all the while wondering how long I could manage. Now that the secret was out, all the emotion I'd held inside wanted to break free and rid my body and mind of everything I'd been holding in.

Cyrus stood with me, holding me securely while I gathered myself, trying to put the genie back in the bottle. It was hard. So very fucking hard. It took several minutes, but I finally managed. The second I tried to step away from him, Cyrus let me go. His arms dropped to his sides, and all the emotion I'd fought so hard to contain threatened to burst free again. Instead, I put my chin up, took a breath, and opened the door to leave.

Cyrus followed me, not letting me far from his side. Once we exited the building, he snagged my hand and led me to his bike. The custom Harley was a thing of beauty. I might not be part of a motorcycle club, but I knew by the way he looked at the bike it was something he took pleasure in. As I stepped close to it, I knew I wanted to be on the back of it. There was no other way to go about it now, I was definitely riding with him this time, but I wanted to be there permanently. And yeah, I knew what being on the back of a man's bike meant to these guys. It meant I was his. Which would likely never happen. Not with Cyrus. And not only because he was tight with my brother.

I sat stiffly, my fists curling into the leather of his cut. He probably wouldn't like it because a biker's cut was almost sacred to him. Bunching the leather might damage it. It didn't surprise me that Cyrus snagged my wrists and pulled my hands away from the vest. What did surprise me was that he pulled me close, urging me to wrap my arms around his waist. The next thing I knew, I pressed the side of my face against his back and flattened my palms against his chest and abdomen. My fingers were splayed wide, wanting to touch every part of him I could. He grunted at me. Approval? Then he started the bike and took off.

We rode for a while. I wasn't ready for him to take me back to the compound and I thought he needed time to think about what had happened. Probably how to let me know all that shit about him being the father of my child was to keep me from being embarrassed any more than I already was in front of the doctor.

After an hour, I was getting tired. I wasn't used to long rides on a bike and though the breeze was wonderful, it was still hot out. I never loosened my hold on him. In fact, the second I realized where we were, I bunched my fists in the front of his shirt, the nervousness I'd been trying to hold off kicking in making me tremble. I was pretty sure what was about to happen. Cyrus was going to let me down as easily as he was capable of. He'd tell me he'd get me back to my brother in Florida or something and that would be it. Once he delivered me to my brother, he'd be out of my life. Again. It shouldn't hurt. It wasn't like he was actually in my life to begin with.

We pulled into the garage and turned off the engine. "Careful of the pipes, darlin'. Don't burn yourself." He got off, but I froze, looking down at the bike helplessly.

"I've never ridden before. I-I don't know what's hot."

"Come here." He stepped close to me and put his arm around my back, his hand under my arm and one under the closest knee. When he lifted, I gasped and put my arms around his neck.

He looked at me, narrowing his gaze as we stood there motionless. I swallowed, not knowing what was wrong other than how I clung to him.

I loosened my arms and he actually growled at me, his grip around me tightening. "Don't."

"I-I... Don't what?"

"Pull away from me. Do *not!*" His voice was harsh, his gaze intense. "Understand?"

"No." I shook my head, tears threatening again.

"I don't understand at all!"

He closed his eyes and shook his head, grunting once. Then he practically dropped me. He reached out to grasp my hips to steady me when I sucked in a breath and stumbled.

"Sorry," he muttered. "Shouldn't 'a done that." Then he turned and stalked out of the garage. "Come on." Now he sounded mad. At me?

I knew I needed to follow him, but the last thing I wanted to do was be anywhere around Cyrus. I needed to hole up in a private space and lick my wounds. I'd been prepared for what the doctor would say, but not for Cyrus to be there, or for him to have already known. Or for him to tell the fucking doctor the baby was his!

"No. I'm just gonna leave. I'm not sure what I came all this way for, but I need to go back home."

He whipped around, walking back in my direction, advancing on me like an angry wildcat. "You said you didn't have a home, so you're not leaving."

"I can go back to Florida. Donovan will let me stay with him until I get things fixed."

"Fixed? What things?" I actually stepped back at the anger in his expression. He closed his eyes, his fists clenched at his side. Taking a deep breath, he shook his head. I was beginning to realize he did that when he was trying to get himself back under control. But why would he be this angry at me?

"My life! Everything got turned topsy-turvy a couple of weeks ago. Then this happened! Why are you angry with me?" I was practically yelling at him, the tears threatening again. I was going to lose it. The only question was if I could get behind closed doors or if the entirety of the compound would be witness to my humiliation.

"I'm not angry with you!" Cyrus raised his voice in proportion to my own. He took another deep breath, giving his head another little shake. "Are you looking to terminate your pregnancy? 'Cause you know this ain't the place."

"What if I am?"

"Then you need to tell me so I can get Stitches to help me find a safe place for you to have the procedure. Either way we have some things to discuss. Come with me." It was an order pure and simple. He held his hand out to me, fully expecting me to take it.

"What's going on with us, Cyrus?"

"Nothing's going on with us," he snapped. "Blade's tryin' his best to help a kid who's dying, and I'm taking care of you so he can concentrate."

If he'd slapped me, I wouldn't have been hurt as much. "So I'm a responsibility."

"I didn't say that. You need someone watchin' over you and I'm fillin' in."

"Well, news flash, asshole! I'm an adult! I can take care of myself. And anyone else who comes along!"

I stormed out of the garage, heading toward the compound. There were several men outside lounging against the building or in chairs on the large patio. Had they heard everything?

Fuck!

I turned abruptly to point a finger at Cyrus, to give him a piece of my mind. He was so hot on my heels, he crashed into me. Again, he enclosed his arms around me. I seemed to be finding myself there a lot. The disturbing thing was, I loved every fucking second of it. But I refused to be a charity case, either financially or emotionally.

"I hate you! You bring me here when you know

I'm struggling to hold it together and attack me! Demanding to know my plans when they're none of your business! And why in the hell would you tell the doctor you're the father of this baby?"

"Not now, Odette." His words were quiet but sharp. "We're fixin' to talk about it all once we get inside." He snagged my arm and I jerked away.

"Fuck you!" I screamed at him, tears streaming down my face. "Fuck! You!"

Cyrus's expression was impassive. He gazed at me steadily, calmly. Like he was the fucking reasonable one when he was the one who snapped first.

"You good, Odette?"

I turned to see Stitches approaching. The other men stood in front of the clubhouse seemingly oblivious when I knew they had to be hanging on every word. My commotion must have alerted the rest of the place because several women filed out of the clubhouse, their expressions ranging from curious to outright gleeful.

"No! I'm not good!" And the dam broke.

Great sobs racked my body as I lost all the control I'd fought so hard to retain. I'd almost made it, too. Had I just kept my mouth shut and followed Cyrus inside, I could have kept all this to myself. Instead, everything -- shock, grief, fear, longing -- all of it came rushing at me with the force and speed of a bullet train. I was eighteen, pregnant, and I had no place to live. No job. No way to survive on my own. I couldn't ask my brother for help because he didn't know about any of my situation, and I didn't want him to.

"Shh... shh..." Strong arms surrounded me, and I clung to the warm body pulling me against it. "I gotcha, honey. I gotcha."

"It all hit her?"

"Yeah. I ain't good at expressin' myself either." That was Cyrus. He was the man who had me. I could feel his chin resting on the top of my head, moving back and forth soothingly. Then his lips as he kissed my hair. I adjusted my grip tighter around his neck, putting myself closer against him. It was the worst possible thing I could do but I couldn't stop myself. I buried my face in his neck and sobbed like a little baby.

"Get her to your room, Cyrus. I'll get her something to calm her down."

"She'll be fine. If I need you, I'll text. She just needs some breathing room and time to process."

"You get tired of the little crybaby, Cyrus, you come see me. Jezlynn'll take care of you."

I stiffened, pushing away from Cyrus until he set me down on my feet. I turned to the woman who'd spoke. It wasn't hard to figure out which one it was. She was front and center, clinging to Cyrus's arm the second he put me down.

"You want him, bitch?" I tilted my head as I studied her. "Well? Do you?"

Jezlynn glanced up at Cyrus who was impassive, then around at the other men surrounding us. One woman giggled, and I thought I heard whispers but couldn't understand what they said.

"Oh, I've had him, little mouse. Several times. I just want to have him again." She gave me a superior smirk, putting her shoulders back and thrusting her breasts. "And again… and again… and again."

I wish I could say I thought really hard about what I did next, but the fact was, I was completely out of control. I threw a punch, putting all my weight behind it. Right in Jezlynn's left tit.

The other woman screamed, stepping away from Cyrus and clutching her arms to her chest. "You bitch!"

"You ain't seen bitch yet." Somehow, my voice was as low and deadly as any badass in any biker compound. It was the same tone of voice my brother, Donovan, had used on the prospect who'd tried to sneak me into the Salvation's Bane compound two years ago.

Jezlynn looked from Cyrus to Stitches. There were other men around us, but I wasn't sure of their names. Other than those two men, I hadn't met the others. I'd seen a few of them, but when I'd made a mad dash out of the compound earlier, I had done my best to keep my head down.

"You guys gonna let her get away with that?" Jezlynn whined. Bitch. "She's not part of Iron Tzars!" The other woman stuck her chin up, though she still held her tit. "I am!"

"You get to live because I haven't put out the word Odette's with me yet. Now you know. Next time you fuckin' touch her or even look at her the wrong way, I'll slit your throat myself."

I blinked up at Cyrus. Though his voice was calm, his gaze was hard. I knew these men were hardasses. I'd heard Donovan say it more than once of the men in Iron Tzars. They were relatively new to Salvation's Bane, only since they'd formed an alliance with Bones in Kentucky and their former president had been recruited by Black Reign. I didn't know the particulars, but I'd heard their recruitment wasn't necessarily a request for Warlock to join. It had been a demand. I saw it now. The men Donovan saw when he looked at them.

Jezlynn gasped and took a step back. Was she really frightened of Cyrus? Surely, she knew he'd never hurt a woman. That wasn't who he was. Was it? 'Course, I'd only met him once, but that was the image I'd built up in my mind. Cyrus as a protector. Not someone who hurt women and children.

"I suggest you take the other women and be someplace else." Another man moved forward, stepping slightly between Cyrus and Jezlynn.

"She's not one of us! Why are so many women invading our space?" She waved a hand at the others behind us. "They're all too scared to say anything, but they think so too! We're part of Tzars! All these women you've brought in from the outside don't belong!"

"Wylde, reach out to another Tzars chapter." I didn't know the man speaking, but everyone looked at him when he spoke. "See if you can find a club who'll take her."

"What?" Jezlynn looked shocked, then angry. "You can't kick me out, Sting!"

"I'm not. I'm getting you transferred. The only reason I'm sending you away instead of ending you is because you've proven loyal to the club for the years you've been here."

"I was here first, Goddamnit!" Jezlynn screamed. "Even before you became a full member, Sting!"

"Yes. You were. Before you became a club whore, you were a lost girl on the streets. Tzars took you in. Thing is, there are very, very few members of any Tzars chapter who were born into the club. Everyone was an outsider at some point. Our women belong here."

"But she's not Cyrus's woman! She's not got her tat or property patch! She's just a girl who got knocked up, then got drunk! Just because she's *with* Cyrus" -- she made air quotes around the word *with* --"doesn't mean she's his old lady!"

"He has the right to explore that option if he wishes. Seems like that's exactly what he's doin'. You don't get a say in this or anything else. You're part of this club, but you ain't a patched member. Go back to your room and stay there until we figure out where we're sendin' you."

Jezlynn shot me a murderous look, but I bared my teeth at her. Maybe if I was a big enough bitch, they'd send me away too.

"You ain't gettin' sent away, so don't think you can act out enough that you will," Sting said before turning to me. There was no doubt he was talking to me. I didn't insult him by pretending I thought he wasn't. "You've had a rough day, Odette. That will only get you so far. My suggestion is for you to swallow your pride and let Cyrus take you up to his room. Stitches says you need food, water, and a ton of sleep. Get all three and you'll feel more like talking things over with Cyrus."

"I'm not his responsibility," I said, trying to keep a rein on both my temper and my tears. "I'm my own person."

"Yes. You are. But Cyrus needs this. The man doesn't ask for much. Frankly, he's never shown any kind of long-term interest in a woman before. As far as I'm concerned, he's gettin' what he wants. That's you."

"What?" I looked from Sting to Cyrus and back. "He doesn't want me. He's looking out for me until my brother isn't too busy to come get me. Even he said so!"

"Yeah?" Sting raised an eyebrow. "Tell yourself that as long as you need to." He jerked his head toward the clubhouse. "I believe you guys have some things to work out, Cyrus."

"We do."

"Make sure she understands everything."

"I may need some help from Wylde with a... project."

Sting smirked. "Yeah. Didn't see that one coming. Give him a name. I'm sure he can track the son of a bitch down. When you're ready, we'll bring the bastard to you."

"Who are you talking about?" I had to know. "My brother?" Had I brought danger to my brother's door? But hadn't Cyrus said they were friends?

"No, lil' bit." Cyrus stepped close to me and, before I realized what he was doing, he scooped me back up into his arms. "Not your brother." He carried me toward the clubhouse.

"Then who?"

"We'll talk about it later. Right now, Sting's right. You need food, water, and care. That first. Then we'll talk."

My emotional outbursts had taken a toll on me. With the adrenaline letdown from the confrontation with Jezlynn, I was weak and shaky. Combine that with all the other emotional turmoil today and I was zonked.

I wrapped my arms around Cyrus's neck and buried my face in his neck. "I'm so sorry, Cyrus. I don't know why I'm such a bitch."

"You're not, honey. You're pregnant. It happens."

I blinked, then pulled back to look at him. "What?"

One side of his lips quirked upward. "Hormones, honey. Hormones."

Had that revelation not just knocked me on my ass I might have slapped his too handsome face. I hadn't even considered the emotional rollercoaster pregnancy might put me on. Instead, I sighed and snuggled into him. I had no idea how long this would last, but Goddamnit, I deserved to have a couple minutes in my fantasy. I'd deal with the repercussions to my self-esteem later. Right now, I wanted to be taken care of by Cyrus. I wanted my dream.

I wanted... *Cyrus.*

Chapter Five
Odette

Cyrus carried me through the common room to the back and up the stairs back to his room. We met more than a few club whores, as they called them, along the way. Most ignored or avoided us. A couple sneered at me, as if they were better than me. Which pissed me the fuck off!

"Retract the claws, lil' bit. Ain't nobody encroachin' on your territory."

"My territory?"

We reached the door to his room. He fumbled to open it but for some reason refused to set me down. Once we were inside, he kicked the door shut and locked it. All the while, I remained in his arms.

"Yeah. Your territory."

I studied him, my eyes narrowing. "And what exactly does that mean? I don't have my own space here."

"Nope. I'm referring to me. I'm your territory. They ain't tryin' to take me from you."

"Now, wait just a Goddamned minute, Cyrus. I never said you were mine. Or even that I wanted you, for that matter."

"You didn't have to." He crossed to the bed and sat down with me now in his lap. "I said it for you."

"Why are you doing this? What's going on that I don't know about? I don't want to be anyone's responsibility, least of all yours!"

He shrugged. "A lot of things. The only thing you need to be concerned about right now is how to get along with me. Believe me. That's enough to keep you occupied for a very long while. And just so you know? I don't view you as a responsibility. It's my privilege to be here for you."

Cyrus brushed a tendril of hair off my forehead. It was an intimate, tender gesture. One I never would have guessed the man capable of. When I thought about it, I had to wonder why I'd seized on him in the first place. I'd known from that brief time at Salvation's Bane when he'd carried me over his shoulder kicking and screaming back to my brother that he was gruff and unbending. When he talked to Donovan, he was every bit the hard-ass. I hadn't seen this side of him before, and I got the feeling not many people had.

"You didn't answer my question. Why are you doing this?"

"Doing what? Holding you in my lap?"

"Taking care of me. Telling the doctor you were my husband. Bringing me to your room. Is it because of how you found me last night? Because I promise I won't be doing that again. It was stupid, but I needed..." I trailed off, not sure how to express myself.

"To find oblivion? A way to escape everything for a little while?" When I nodded, he smiled gently. "I get it, lil' bit. But you're right. You won't be doing it again. Not while I'm alive."

"Cyrus --"

"No, Odette. I'm serious." He shifted his grip and turned me to face him, straddling his hips. My knees were on the bed beside him, my hands on his shoulders to balance myself. Cyrus pulled me down so that I sat fully on him. When I felt his cock twitch beneath my pussy, I sucked in a breath.

"Oh, God," I breathed.

"Hush, lil' bit. Listen to me." He put both his hands on my face, framing it as he gazed at me. "What happens with this baby is your choice. I'll be here to support you no matter what. But there are some things you need to accept and understand." He waited until I nodded slightly. My breath came quicker and I had to bite my cheek to keep from whimpering. "First, you're gonna tell me why you came to Evansville. Second, I want you to let me help you figure out what you're going to do."

"You said it was my choice."

"It is, baby. Completely your choice. But no matter what you choose, you're gonna need someone in your corner helpin' you. That's me. You tell me what you want, and I'll make it a reality. No matter what it is. Understand?"

"Not really."

"Then let me spell this part out right now. You're with me now, Odette. We're a couple. You're gonna be my old lady and stay here with me. I'll deal with your brother, but this is a done thing. You just need to tell Sting you're good with it, and Wylde will take care of everything else."

I barked out a laugh. "Sounds like you're ordering me to marry you, or something."

"Ain't askin' and takin' the chance you'll say no. I already tried to bully Wylde into filin' the paperwork to make us legally married, but he refused until Sting gave him the go-ahead. I don't like the word 'no', so I avoid it any way I can."

"How convenient. For you." I couldn't help the smile tugging at my lips. Inappropriate as it was, the man was just too cute for words. Beneath that gruff exterior was a man who was slightly insecure. At least with his feelings. Which, I was sure, he'd never admit.

"I like the path of least resistance. Easier for everyone."

"That it?"

"Nope. You're also gonna tell me what son of a

bitch knocked you up, then let you leave."

"I don't think that's your business, Cyrus." I shrugged. "It's over between me and him. Not sure there was ever really anything to begin with."

"He part of Salvation's Bane?"

My laugh sounded bitter even to my own ears. "No. If he was, things would have been different. Donovan would have seen to it."

"You want the guy back?" Though his question sounded harsh, I thought there was a hint of vulnerability in his eyes. I had to really think about this one.

Cyrus was a conundrum. I'd heard my brother say more than once the man didn't get other people's emotions. That he had a form of autism called Asperger's Syndrome or something. I didn't understand it all, but the basic gist was that he didn't always understand other people's emotions and how he might affect them. Also, he had trouble figuring out his own emotions. He didn't like change and he liked things strictly regimented. So far I hadn't seen much of those traits, but he did seem to be hyper-focused on me for some reason. It was definitely something I needed to look into if I intended on letting him into my life.

"No. Not even a little, Cyrus."

He relaxed, but his facial expression didn't change. "Good. 'Cause it ain't happening. Not even if you want it."

"But you said whatever I wanted you'd make happen."

"Don't twist my words, girl. That was with regard to the baby. This is something I absolutely will not budge on. He had his chance. You're gonna tell me what happened, but no matter what, he couldn't keep you. Now it's my turn."

"I can't pretend a relationship with you isn't something I want, so I'm not even going to try."

"Good. We'll settle that with Sting when we're done here."

"You do realize we've just met. I mean, in any meaningful way. Last time I remember hanging upside down while you lectured me all the way to my brother's office. While I got a great view of your ass, the conversation wasn't very meaningful."

"Yeah? Tell me why you came to Evansville instead of taking your problem to your brother for help with it?"

I swallowed. Yeah. He had me there. "Look. I admit it's a bit childish, but you made an impression on me." I couldn't believe I was about to say this. Even admitting it to myself was embarrassing. It sounded like a schoolgirl crush even to myself. "I guess I fixated on you. I had no intention of seeking you out, but when I got in my car and started driving, this is where I ended up. I never would have bothered you with my fucked-up life."

"So? I found you. Now that I have, what did you hope would happen?"

"In reality? Nothing."

"Ain't talkin' about reality, lil' bit. When you thought about findin' me, what did you want to happen?"

I closed my eyes and took a breath. "I wanted you to take over. To tell me what to do and how to fix everything." I knew I sounded weak and helpless, but it was the truth. And for some stupid reason, I wanted to give this man the truth. No matter how much it embarrassed me.

"OK. That wasn't so hard, was it?"

I shook my head. "I can't let you. This is my

mess."

"And I'm making it mine. You didn't ask me. I volunteered."

"You've asked me all kinds of questions. Now I want to ask you one." He opened his mouth, probably to tell me I had to wait until I'd answered all of his, but I refused to go on until I had my answer. "Why, Cyrus? Why would you volunteer to take all this on?"

"Because you need help."

"You can turn me over to my brother. He'll help me."

"No, Odette!" His anger was palpable. Quick and hot. He didn't like that idea one bit. Curious. "You're not getting help from your brother unless he's a resource we use. I'm gonna be the one to take care of you."

"By all accounts, you don't play nice with others. You don't like people in your space, and you like a strictly regimented existence. Just so you know, I'm a chaotic mess. Literally. My place used to look like a whirlwind went through it. Drove Steve crazy."

"Steve the man who got you pregnant?"

I winced. Yeah. Hadn't meant to give that away. "If I say no, will you forget you ever heard that name?"

"Nothing wrong with my memory, honey. Last name."

"Why?"

"Look. If you're going to keep the baby, he's going to sign away his rights so I can claim the child. Also, I'm not going to have you constantly worrying he'll figure it out and try to come after you for money or some shit by threatening to take the baby away. I'll find it out one way or another. Wylde will be upset if he finds out you could have told him everything up front and he had to go digging anyway."

"Fine. Steve Gleeson's his name. He's fifteen years older than me, and I had no clue he was married. He said he was widowed."

Cyrus's gaze pinned me. "Must have been convincing."

"I fell for a classic con. He claimed to love me, but there was always a reason he couldn't take me out in public with him. I was only with him for a couple of months before I finally figured it out." I sighed. "OK, so I didn't exactly figure it out. I happened to run into him and his wife. And their two young kids."

"When was this?"

"Three days before I got here. Two days after I found out I might be pregnant." I closed my eyes, wanting to cuddle into Cyrus but not sure I had the right. Or that he'd want me to take comfort in him after hearing this. "You have no idea how hard it is to admit what I did. I slept with a married man. Got pregnant with his child."

"You said he told you his wife was dead."

"He did, but I should have known."

"How? How were you supposed to have known he was lying to you?"

I shrugged. "I don't know."

"Because there was no way for you to know. You were with him two months?"

"Yes."

"I take it he doesn't know about the baby."

"I didn't even know for sure until today, Cyrus. I saw them at a movie theater. He saw me and the second he met my gaze, I knew. I was going to leave but decided that no, I was there to watch a picture I'd been wanting to see for months. I wasn't letting him run me off. So, I bought my ticket and went to stand in line for concessions. I tried not to watch them. I tried so hard, but it hurt. More that I'd been played than from the loss of him, but it still hurt. As I was headed into the theater, he met me in the hall. Accused me of following him and told me his wife would never believe a little whore like me if I tried to tell her he was fucking me. He said I wasn't getting one cent of his money, no matter what I threatened, but I swear, Cyrus. I didn't threaten to tell his wife or break up his happy home in any way. I don't know anything about any money he has, and if I did I wouldn't want it. I wasn't even going to confront him at all. If I'd told him I was pregnant, not only would he not have believed me, he'd have blamed me."

"Why didn't you insist on protection?" All his questions were asked matter-of-factly. Like he could care less what the answers were, but his intense gaze said otherwise. He was extremely interested in my answers.

"I did. He was my…" I winced, unable to finish that sentence.

"Your… what? Tell me, Odette."

"The first guy I ever had sex with."

Cyrus took several breaths. His hands had slid down my body to rest on the tops of my thighs. Given the way the muscle in his jaw ticked, I expected his grip on my legs to tighten painfully. Instead, he simply slid his palms up and down my bare legs in a soothing gesture. It was funny how much he calmed me while fighting his own internal war.

"He know that?"

"Yeah. He used a condom the first few times we had sex, but made no secret he wanted to take me without it. I always said no, but one time, he pulled it off before we had sex. I thought it felt different but didn't know until afterward."

"Did you confront him?"

"I was shocked. He just laughed and told me not to worry, he was clean."

"He know you weren't on birth control?"

I nodded my head. "I don't think he cared. Looking back, I'm pretty sure it was all a power thing."

"Oh, I'm sure of it."

We were silent for a long time. Just staring at each other. My hands still rested on his shoulders, though I occasionally moved my hand to toy with the hair at the back of his neck. I couldn't seem to stop touching him. I wanted the right to explore every inch of him. The heavy muscles of his shoulders and arms tempted me in ways I couldn't even begin to process.

"Now what?" I asked softly.

"Now you get what you came for. I'm takin' over and helping you through this. You're in the six-week window if you want an abortion, but you'll need to tell me now if that's what you want. I'll probably have to get Wylde and Stitches both to pull some strings to make it happen in Indiana fast enough to accommodate you, but we can do it."

I frowned, thinking seriously about it for the first time. Did I want an abortion? "No," I sighed. "I don't want to do that. Not really."

"Good. Next thing is to make you my old lady and my wife. Easily done. Wylde probably has everything ready to go. He's just waiting on the OK from Sting. You just have to tell him that's what you want." He hesitated, looking at me almost guiltily. "There are a couple things you need to know, though. Not that it will make a difference. You're still mine. I don't give up what's mine."

"That's not cryptic or anything. Tell me."

"When a Tzar takes an old lady, she has to get

inked with her man's property patch. You can see the other old ladies' tats to get an idea. They're each unique to the woman, and the men have all adopted the practice of getting a matching tat on their left ring finger."

"Like a wedding band or something?"

"Yeah. Exactly."

"That actually sounds rather sweet. But what happens if they get divorced?"

"That's the second thing. There is no divorce in our club."

I frowned. "Why not?"

"We're not like Salvation's Bane or Bones, or even Black Reign. Iron Tzars do things we don't want to get out. To anyone. We have our own code we live by, but we're not always on the right side of the law."

"No surprise there. Neither is Bane."

"Compared to us, they are. This club has a rich tradition of righting wrongs, no matter the cost. We don't hurt innocents, and we always make sure of what we're doing so there are no mistakes. The reason for the no-divorce rule is that men talk to their women and vice versa. In all the years since Iron Tzars have been in existence, we've never had a secret get out of our gates. That's because every person affiliated with us from patched member to prospect, or old lady to club whore is completely loyal to us. They don't leave."

"Sting just sent Jezlynn away."

"He's sending her to a different chapter. We have them all over the country. All over the world, really. As long as there isn't a loyalty problem, all the chapters work together to make sure all our members and women have a home in one of our chapters." There was something he was leaving out, and I wasn't really sure I wanted to know it all. Still, my big mouth opened and out it came.

"As long as there isn't a loyalty problem. What exactly does that mean?"

Did I imagine he winced? "If someone inside is disloyal to the club, if they breach our trust or try to leave once they've been privy to any of our secrets, they're dealt with by the club. Permanently."

It took a minute for that to sink in. When it did, I found myself shaking my head. "I don't think I want to be part of that, Cyrus."

"Why not? It's not like you're leaving, and I don't believe for a minute you'd betray me or the club."

I tried to get off his lap, but he slid his hands around to grip my ass and pull me back. "Let me up, Cyrus."

"Not happening," he growled. "You sit here with me, and we work this out. This is how it works."

"You're talking about having me killed if I try to leave you! Cyrus, we've known each other less than a day! What the fuck?"

His chin jutted up. "You sayin' I can't keep you satisfied?"

"I'm saying we don't even know if we like each other! Hell, half the time I'm with you I want to kick you in the balls!"

"And the other half?" He raised an eyebrow.

"Cyrus --"

"No, Odette. We have chemistry."

"Sure. I feel safe with you. You're the sexiest man I've ever met. You're over the top protective. But you're also a complete asshole without even trying."

There it was. That flash of vulnerability I'd had a glimpse of a couple of times.

"I know I'm different. I don't always understand how my words or actions affect other people's emotions. Hell, half the time I don't understand my own, but I know without a doubt I want you with me."

"My brother said you had Asperger's Syndrome."

He shrugged. "Yeah. It's not a bad form of it, and I can mostly control myself. But I still have problems relating to others. Usually when I don't want to relate to them."

I couldn't help but grin. "I take it you don't want to most of the time."

"Maybe. Ain't ever met someone I felt a need to relate to. Until the first time I saw you." Cyrus didn't have many expressions and the ones he did were very subtle. Just in the time I'd known him, though, I was noticing a few. He was telling me the truth. On all counts.

"You realize I'm way younger than you. Right? At least a good ten years."

"Yep. Still want you, Odette. Don't think you're gonna talk your way out of this. You're not. It's only a matter of time until I convince you to go all in with me. That doesn't change the fact that you're still gonna be my old lady."

"You don't love me, Cyrus," I said softly. "I can't marry a man who doesn't love me."

I knew the second I said the words it was a mistake. "But you love me."

"I didn't say that."

"You didn't *not* say it either. You said you couldn't marry a man who didn't love you. That implies you'd have to love him too. It also implies that you love me since you didn't specify you'd have to love me to marry me."

"Has anyone ever told you you're damned frustrating?"

"All the damned time, baby."

"I don't love you. But I could see myself loving you given enough time."

He studied me before shaking his head. "I can't tell if you're lying or not. I'm going with not since this is moving faster than you're comfortable with."

"What about you? Could you see yourself loving me?"

For the first time since I'd met him, Cyrus didn't have an answer. In fact, he looked confused as all get out. Like he didn't understand the question.

"I'm not sure."

"Ouch."

"No," he said hastily. "That's not what I mean. I'm not sure, you know, what that is." He cleared his throat, looking away. Embarrassed? "Love."

"I'm surprised you'd admit that."

"I'll never keep things from you, Odette. I want to give you what you need. I'm just not sure how with this."

"Then we should slow down."

Immediately he got that stubborn mien that secretly made me smile. "We're not slowing down. This is happening."

I couldn't help myself. I laughed. Seriously. The man was like a kid with a new toy he absolutely refused to give up.

"This isn't a decision I can make on the fly."

"Like I said. There's no decision for you to make. You wanted me to take over? That's what I'm doing."

"Life or death, Cyrus. That means this is one thing you're not taking over. Not yet. What if you abuse me? Mentally or physically. What if you cheat?

What if I wake up one morning and realize that I simply go, 'God, I can't stand the fact that you have to have everything in the house just so, and it's making me crazy that I can't leave my dirty underwear on the bathroom floor for more than the fifteen minutes it takes me to shower?' What if I can't stand living with you because you're stubborn and need to control everything around you, because I can see both those traits coming out in spades right now."

"I hurt you in any way, but especially if I hit you or berate you or humiliate you or any other of a million things a person could do to mentally abuse someone, you go to Sting or any member of the Iron Tzars. Or any of the old ladies. Sting will deal with me and the whole club will protect you. If I ever hit you, my life will be forfeit. No questions asked."

"That gives me a lot of power."

"It does. But if you were the kind of person to have me killed in cold blood, I wouldn't want you with me."

"Again, Cyrus. You don't know me. Which is my whole point here. Twenty-four hours isn't nearly enough time."

"It is for me. If you'd let yourself turn off your brain and act on instinct, I think you'd realize it's enough time for you too."

Chapter Six
Cyrus

What the everlasting fuck was I thinking? Taking Odette as my old lady? She needed someone to protect her. To protect her baby -- assuming she decided to keep it. I was the best protector she could find, which was why I volunteered.

I could keep her and the baby safe. From every-fucking-body. And when I found that asshole who'd played her, then knocked her up, I was gonna make it so he never did it to another young woman ever again. Assuming I let him live.

Yes. That was my plan. I was committing to taking care of a friend's sister and her child. I might never be able to give her the love she probably needed, but I could give her a stable home, a faithful man, and as much pleasure as she wanted.

Which brought up another question. Had that bastard who'd lied to her made her feel good?

Yeah. No. Wasn't touching that. I got a pain in my chest thinking about her with someone else. Not happening again. She was mine.

The moment the thought entered my mind, I knew I meant it. I might not deal well with emotions, but I knew what I wanted. This possessiveness was something new. I'd never been possessive over anything other than, perhaps, my bike. What I felt for Odette surpassed anything I had even felt before. I'd say it bordered on the obsessive, but it went way beyond that. I'd passed obsessive a long damn time ago. I was in the realm of stalker but wasn't about to back off.

"I'm not saying you're right, Cyrus, but yeah. I feel safe with you. I know you'd never intentionally hurt me. How do I know that?" She gave a little chuckle. "No fucking clue. I just can't believe my brother would be close with someone who wasn't a good person."

"At the risk of cutting my own throat, don't kid yourself. I'm not a nice man, Odette. But I will protect you with my life and do everything in my power to make you happy."

She was still straddling my lap. My cock was a living thing between us. There was no way she could fail to notice it, but she only stiffened once -- when I first positioned her over me.

"You need food and rest," I said, not wanting to let her out of my arms but knowing I couldn't keep her with me like this forever. "You want a shower while I round you up something?"

"Yeah. I think that'd be nice."

"Good. I think the women got you some bathroom stuff, and I had a couple prospects retrieve your things from the crappy hotel you were staying at." If there was disapproval in my voice, it was deserved. The place she was staying at was in a bad part of town and probably had rodents and insects scurrying around.

"It was what I could comfortably afford for the longest amount of time."

"No excuses, Odette. I think that's three I owe you."

She gave me a blank look, like she didn't remember my promise to spank her. "Three what?"

"Spankings. I mean to deliver those the second it's official that you're mine."

"Not a very good incentive for me to tell Sting I agree. Besides, I haven't done anything to deserve a spanking." God, she was sexy when she fought me.

Didn't mean she'd get her way about something like this.

"No? You got drunk. In a bar. On your own. What would have happened if my brothers hadn't dragged my ass there?"

"I'd have been all right."

I snorted. "You passed out in my arms, Odette. You literally fell into my arms, sniffed me, then passed out."

"Only because I knew it was you."

"Little liar. That's four, by the way."

"What is it with you and spankings?"

I grinned at her. A genuine grin. I wasn't sure when the last time I felt the *need* to smile. The sensation didn't feel as awkward as I thought it might. In fact, with Odette wrapped around me like she was, it felt right. "Maybe I just love your ass."

She raised an eyebrow. "You do, huh?"

"Oh yeah." I slid my hands around to squeeze the fleshy globes gently for emphasis. "I certainly do."

"Even if you do, that's still only one."

"Yeah? You lied to me. First in the doctor's office and then putting yourself in danger by staying at that fleabag motel. Then you lied just now when you said you knew I was the man who had you when you fell off the stage last night. You were too drunk to know your own name let alone recognize a man you hadn't seen in two years." The more I thought about what could have happened last night if I hadn't been there, the more my chest tightened and it was hard to breathe.

"Cyrus?"

"What!" I snapped at her, not meaning to, but the thought of something happening to her was not sitting well with me.

She blinked several times, her gaze not leaving mine. Then her features softened. "I'm fine, Cyrus. Nothing happened to me. You saved me."

"Damned straight I did," I muttered, clearing my throat. "And you'll never do anything like that again. You want to get drunk, you do it with me watching over you."

"That was the only time I've ever done anything like that. I knew what I was doing, yet I guess I didn't, all at the same time."

We stared at each other a long moment. The band tightening around my chest eased somewhat and I could breathe a little easier. Odette brought her small hand to my cheek and stroked my beard in a soothing gesture. "I really am OK, you know."

"And I intend to keep you that way."

She hesitated a second, then leaned in and brushed her lips over mine tentatively. The second she did, my world exploded.

I'd kissed a few women in my lifetime, most of them in my younger days before I decided I really didn't like the act of kissing. It was too intimate, and I didn't like intimacy. Intimacy implied something more than just sex. Since I first became self-aware, I knew I wasn't like other people. I didn't have the same reactions to certain situations as other people. Even anger was usually over other people's stupidity or frustration when I couldn't make someone understand me, not at the situation itself. I was fully aware I'd been angry several times over the last day because of the danger and/or disrespect to Odette. The fact she wouldn't fully commit to me now was another frustration, even if her objections made perfect sense. The animal inside me recognized her as mine and wasn't taking no for an answer.

Now, with her lips pressed to mine, another emotion I wasn't acquainted with shot through me. Lust, hard and mean, punched through me like a dagger to the heart. I was done. God help anyone who came between me and Odette because she was fucking *mine.*

I wrapped my arms around her tightly, holding her against me as I deepened the kiss. Sweeping my tongue into her mouth, I took her taste inside me, reveling in the fact that I'd get to taste those delectable lips anytime I wanted.

She moaned, opening her mouth, letting me take what I had to have. The problem was, the more I had, the more I wanted. She was like a drug. Potent and addictive. If that were true, I wanted to keep my addiction because Odette was providing the sweetest, most wonderful sensations I'd ever experienced.

I pulled her closer to me so my cock was mashed against her between her legs. The heat of her through her shorts was scorching, her pussy already wanting something she wasn't ready for mentally or emotionally. She was right that she needed more time. I was sure she was still feeling the effects of what Steve Gleeson had put her through. I didn't in any way want her to equate what that man had taken from her with me.

"Cyrus..." My whispered name on her lips only made me more possessive of her. I growled as I continued to kiss her, moving her over the ridge of my cock in a steady rhythm. "What is this?" She shivered, moving her hips faster and faster as she rubbed over my cock.

"Feel good?"

"Oh, God! Yes! Help me!"

I scooted us back on the bed and rolled so she

was underneath me. Odette tightened her legs around me, lifting herself to me while I situated us. She wasn't passive by any measure. Odette thrust her hips at me, rocking over my cock in a maddening glide that threatened to unman me. And there was no way that was fucking happening. At least, not until she came. After that all bets were off.

"Take what you need, Odette," I growled. Sweat dotted her skin and I couldn't help but put my face in her neck and lick.

Odette squealed and stiffened. Then she screamed. I felt her pussy quivering against my cock as she came, the thin shorts she wore not an adequate buffer between us. As much as I wanted to follow her, I decided in that moment I would not come until I was deep inside her. Then I'd fill her so full she'd never forget who she belonged to.

I let her ride out her pleasure while I kissed and nipped the skin of her neck and shoulder. I wanted to strip her bare and continue what we'd started, but I didn't think now was the right time. Soon. But not now.

When she stopped moving, I pulled back to look at her. There was a bemused smile on her face and a dazed look in her eyes.

"Wow," she whispered.

"Haven't you ever orgasmed before?"

"I thought I had." She shook her head. "I'm rethinking that assessment."

I barked out a startled laugh. "There's much, much more where that came from, lil' bit. I'll take you down that road as many times as you'll let me."

She laid a hand on the side of my face before pulling me back to her for another kiss. I could get lost in those kisses and never find my way out.

"Thank you, Cyrus. I'll never forget this moment."

"Damn straight you'll never forget it." I gave her a hard kiss before pushing myself off her. I snagged her hand and pulled her up. "Go take a shower. I'll bring back something to eat, then you can rest."

She gave me a shy look, like she was unsure of herself. "Will you stay with me? I-I mean, for a little while?"

"Honey, I'll stay as long as you want me."

With a nod, Odette turned and went into the bathroom.

I stood there a long while, debating on whether or not to follow her and shower with her but thought better of it. She needed care. Not a horny biker trying to fuck her. That could come later. After all, we had all the time in the world.

* * *

Odette

I took my time in the shower to get my wits back. I'd give Cyrus one thing. He certainly knew what he was doing with regard to sex. Steve had been my first sexual partner. While I'd never orgasmed with him during sex, I'd experimented playing with myself using porn videos on my phone as a guide. I'd found some pleasure this way. But nothing like what had just happened.

As I thought about it while warm water cascaded over me, my knees trembled and I shivered. My pussy clenched, wanting to be filled. I ached with need even though I'd orgasmed not ten minutes before.

If there was anyone who knew better than to surrender to a man because he showed a physical interest, it was me. Yet, I found myself doing just that. I wanted what Cyrus was offering. Wanted to be his woman. His wife. I wasn't sure about the whole not being able to leave thing, but that concern didn't really seem important. If Cyrus kept me happy, if he took care of me like he'd been doing the last day, I knew I'd never want to leave.

Then there was my brother. That was the one thought that finally sobered me. Donovan was going to be furious. With this whole situation. Even though me and Cyrus had talked about him several times, when he found out where I was and why I was here, he was going to lose his mind. I might well get that spanking Cyrus threatened. Not only had I not told him I was in trouble, but I'd taken off on my own without telling him where I was going.

I didn't live with my brother or anywhere near the Salvation's Bane compound, but he always checked on me. Every single day. I answered his calls but always gave him some song and dance about where I was. He wasn't nosy and all in my business, so as long as I answered my phone, he didn't push. To say he wasn't going to be happy with me was a vast understatement.

With a sigh, I turned off the water and grabbed a towel. I dried and dressed before brushing out my hair and exiting the bathroom. When I did, Cyrus stood from where he sat at the small table in his room. He had a plate of green beans, corn, mashed potatoes, and a pork chop waiting on me. His chin was up, but he looked uncomfortable.

"I wasn't sure what you liked, but Stitches said this would be healthy for you." Was he nervous about what he'd brought me to eat? I was beginning to realize Cyrus was doing his best to get this right. He was determined to get this right and wasn't sure how to go about it. I could tell by how his normal confidence was absent. He seemed unsure of himself. He was born for the role of protector, but trying to be a nurturer. I thought it was adorable. Not that I'd ever tell him that. That would definitely get my ass spanked.

"Thank you. I'm sure it's delicious."

"Blaze made it. Said it wasn't much, but it was quick. Said not to hold it against him."

I smiled as I took a seat at the table. "Please thank him for his hard work."

He nodded as I dug in.

Ambrosia!

Who'd have thought such a simple meal could be so freaking *good*? The corn and potatoes were rich and buttery, the pork chop tender and perfectly cooked, the flavor strong. The beans went perfectly with the combination, though I wasn't overly fond of green beans. It all was so delicious I couldn't seem to stop eating. Before I knew it, I'd cleaned my plate and glanced around for more. I hadn't even noticed the glass of milk sitting beside my plate. The second I did, I drank it down.

I realized I probably looked like a crazy person, wolfing down my food like I was starved. When I looked over at Cyrus, he was grinning from ear to ear. It was a strange but good look on him. One I hoped to see on him often because of something I'd done to put it there.

Was this love? I didn't know. My parents had died three years ago in a boating accident. It was part of the reason I'd tried to sneak into the Bane compound with that prospect two years before. It was a rebellion of sorts. A need to be noticed. A cry for attention. I missed them both terribly. It was an aching wound I was sure would never heal. I wanted to fill that void with someone else. The prospect hadn't been that person, but I thought Cyrus might be.

No. That wasn't true. He wasn't a substitute for what I'd lost. It was why I questioned my feelings for him now. No. What I was starting to feel for Cyrus was vastly different. At least, I thought it was. It was hard to tell because I'd built him up in my mind to be the great love of my life. After Steve, I didn't really trust my judgment anymore.

"I can get you more. Blaze will be happy you want more."

"No. I think I'm good." I smiled at him. "Thank you, Cyrus. For everything. I'm sorry I was such a bitch and gave you such a hard time. You kept me safe and got me medical attention. Both today and last night. I want you to know I appreciate all you did for me."

"You never have to thank me for takin' care of you, honey. I'll always take care of you."

He cleared the dishes while I stood and stretched. Now that I was full, I really wanted that nap. "I've decided the night life isn't for me." I grinned when he gave me a skeptical look. "Really! I'm exhausted."

"Thought you might be. Come on. I'll lie down with you."

I stripped down to my underwear and the T-shirt I was wearing and crawled under the covers. It was only one in the afternoon, but I knew there was no way I could stay awake much longer.

Cyrus lay down beside me and pulled me into his arms. I laid my head on his chest and breathed him in. He was everything I'd ever wanted. Not only was he strong and handsome, but he was caring and protective as hell. I could see myself falling head over heels in love with him. It really wouldn't take much considering how much I'd fantasized about him.

"Cyrus?" I was so sleepy, my words were slurred, but I needed to get this out before I passed out.

"Yeah, baby."

"Please don't break my heart."

"Never. You'll always be safe with me. Every part of you."

I took a deep breath, then let it out. The last thing I heard was Cyrus's fervent promise. "I'll kill to keep you safe. Body and heart."

Chapter Seven
Cyrus

Relationship shit was hard. Mainly because there was another person I had to let make decisions when I was better suited for it. Odette was as stubborn as I knew she would be. Though I tried to ignore how much of a turn-on it was, every time she stuck that chin up to tell me what for, I got hard as a fucking rock. Which meant I'd spent a lot of time in the shower jerking off because I didn't think she wanted me throwing myself at her. Sure, I'd gotten her off and I slept with her every night and held her when she napped, but that was different.

It had been a week since I'd found her. I'd been in touch with Blade, who'd cheerfully promised to cut off my balls if I fucked his sister. I hadn't yet fucked her, but it was because it wasn't what Odette needed right now. Not because a man named Blade, who was a skilled physician -- and almost as big a badass as I was -- had promised to castrate me.

"Cyrus?" Odette stood next to me, laying her small hand on my shoulder as she looked up into my face. She was acting more rationally over the past few days. Good food, plenty of water, and lack of alcohol had vastly improved her mood. Well, that and a whole lot of Goddamned sleep. The woman had slept nearly sixteen hours the first couple of days she'd been with me after the doctor had given her that first check-up and confirmed the news that she was pregnant. Now, she was more relaxed. She smiled more. And her moods had stabilized. Mostly.

"Yeah, baby. Everything OK?"

"Yes! Better than OK." She gave me a soft smile… only for it to fade. She looked away, biting her lip.

"Don't say everything's OK when it's not, Odette." I gently grasped her chin and turned her to me. "I thought we were past that."

"We are. And everything really is fine. It's just..."

"Tell me what you need. I can't fix it if I don't know what it is."

She gave me an exasperated look. "You know, you could make things sound like less of an order and more like you were concerned and want me to tell you."

I tilted my head at her, confused. "Why the hell would I do that? You need something, you tell me. That's your job. You should tell me whether I ask you or not."

"Cyrus, shut up."

I blinked. She was smiling so I didn't think she was irritated at me. More amused from the look of it, though why I had no idea. I did as she told me, not saying a word.

She sighed, letting her hand slide from my face to my chest where she patted it once before settling. "Look. You said we were going to be together. Right?"

"Right." I gave her one crisp nod. She was getting it and I was proud she was. It meant fewer misunderstandings by everyone.

"So? Are you ever going to have sex with me?" As she asked her question, she stiffened. "Or do you not want sex to be part of this? I thought with what happened last week --"

"Of course, I want sex to be part of this." I pulled her into my arms, wrapping a hand around her head to press the side of her face against my chest. I kissed the top of her head and tried to keep my body from reacting to her words. "I want it with every fiber of my fuckin' being!" The thought of taking her to the bed, stripping her down to her delectable skin, then fucking her senseless gave me a hard-on to beat all hard-ons.

"But you haven't done anything since that first time. You know. After my meltdown and... altercation with that club girl."

"No, I haven't. But I can assure you the shower has been my fuckin' best friend."

She pulled back to look up at me. "What?"

"Odette, I want you more than I want my next fuckin' breath, but I wasn't sure you were ready for it."

Her expression softened. "I appreciate you looking out for me, but I'm more than ready, Cyrus."

"Are you sure? Because I won't be letting you go once we do this."

"Oh? So if we don't have sex, you'll let me go back to my brother?"

Immediately, I had a visceral reaction to that simple statement. My heart accelerated, my stomach clenched, and a wave of possessive anger at the possibility she'd leave me threatened to have me snapping at her again, like I'd done several times since I'd met her. I wasn't angry at her. Exactly. Only at the possibility that she'd leave me. Or that she might want to leave me.

I'd been trying my hardest, damnit! I'd tried to anticipate her needs, to make sure she got enough rest. I'd introduced her to the club's old ladies in hopes they'd ease any fears she had about the situation I was demanding of her. I'd done everything I could to prove to her I'd provide a comfortable, giving environment for her. And there was still a chance she would leave me?

"Never! Fuckin' never, Odette!"

I pulled her back to me, securing her against my chest. It wasn't until I realized that she was shaking that I let her go, fearing I'd squeezed her too tightly. Or, worse, frightened her. "Odette?"

When she looked up, there was a smile on her face and I almost fell to my knees in relief. And because the sight of this girl smiling was the most glorious thing I'd ever witnessed. Except maybe the look on her face when she came.

She giggled. Actually fucking giggled! "I'm teasing you, Cyrus."

"Teasing?"

"Yeah. You know. Teasing. Poking fun at you for being so possessive. Playing."

"Why..." I shook my head, not understanding. "Why would you do that?"

"Because you need to not take everything so seriously. You're an old man. You're gonna give yourself an ulcer -- EEK!"

I bent and put my shoulder in her abdomen to heft her up and carry her to the bed. "Playing?" I swatted her ass. "Playing? I'll show you playing, little girl."

She let loose a peal of laughter as I tossed her to the bed and whipped off my shirt. Odette was so fucking beautiful it made my chest hurt. Everything about her was sweetness and light to me. Well, except her prickly temper, but I still put it down to hormones. Also, it kind of turned me on, except when it was because I'd done something to really displease her. I didn't like that at all.

I was so fucked.

She scooted back on the bed, like she was trying to get away from me. So I snagged her ankle and pulled her back before digging my fingers into her sides to tickle her.

Odette squealed and laughed, wiggling beneath me when I covered her small body with my own big one. I buried my face in her neck and blew a raspberry, making her cry out even more.

"Might tickle you till you pee. How's that for playing, huh?"

We continued that way for another minute or two while I maneuvered her more to the center of the bed before I completely blanketed her body with mine. I tunneled my fingers through her hair and put her head where I wanted it as I stared down at her. She looked up at me, breathless with pink cheeks and a big smile and I… was… done.

I took her mouth in a kiss I'd wanted to be tender and gentle, but the second she thrust her tongue into my mouth to tangle with mine, I lost any control I had along with the ability to take her slowly this first time.

She moaned, arching her back to thrust her breasts more firmly against my chest. Her legs circled my hips in an attempt to rub against the ridge of my clock. Her nails dug into my shoulders before scoring down my back. The little bite of pain planting her mark of ownership on my body was the biggest turn-on I'd ever experienced. Lust was strong and vicious. Like it always seemed to be when I was around her.

I moved my body to give her the friction she needed, but I wasn't about to let her come yet. Not this time.

"So fuckin' hot, aren't you?"

"Are you going to fuck me now?"

"Oh yeah, baby. I'm damned well gonna fuck you. Don't think this is a one-time thing, though."

"I certainly hope it's not a one-time thing." She grinned.

"I mean it, Odette. This is your commitment to me. I'll fuckin' hold you to it."

"Cyrus --"

"I told you, baby. This is happening. Whether or not we fuck now. I tried to give you time but you went and asked for it, so this is you accepting me. Instead of waiting another week or so, I'm makin' you mine now. I'll get your cut and have Ace get ready to do your property tattoo. It's same as a done thing."

She actually rolled her eyes at me, but there was still a smile on her face. "How about we table that discussion for after you fuck me?" That perfectly arched eyebrow raising made my cock ache even worse.

Instead of answering her, I shoved her shirt over her chest to cup her tits through her bra. "Always knew you were trouble."

"Never said I wasn't."

"Don't think I've forgotten about the spankin' I owe you. Might be time to follow through."

Was that heat in her eyes? I wasn't sure. Could be fear, but I didn't think so. I hoped not. Because my hand was itching to deliver on my promise. And that thought was all I could take.

I shoved her bra over her tits and took one nipple into my mouth. Her breasts were small and exquisite, the nipples long, dusky pink, and absolutely delicious. I rubbed the nub along the roof of my mouth with my tongue while I pinched and twisted the other gently.

"Ahh!" She cried out, holding my head to her chest with her little hands fisted in my hair. I rubbed my beard over her chest as I continued to suck and tease her ripe nipples. Over and over, I alternated between one breast then the other. It didn't take long for sweat to make her skin a slippery, silky playground for me to explore with my hands, mouth, and the rest of my body. The feel of her smooth skin over my hair roughened chest was the most amazing thing I'd ever felt.

It wasn't long before she became impatient, shoving me away so she could pull her shirt completely off and shimmy out of her shorts. More than once she almost nailed me in the balls when I refused to move from between her legs as she struggled to get her shorts and panties off. I loved watching her like this, knowing she was impatient for me to fuck her.

I knelt there between her legs while she gripped my hips and tried to pull me closer. "What are you waiting for? Get your pants off."

With a smirk, I pulled my wallet out of my back pocket and tossed a condom on the bed beside her. "This is your one shot, Odette. I'll use a condom until you say otherwise, but once that bridge is crossed, there's no going back. Get me?"

She cocked her head to the side, her eyes wide. It was a shit move on my part, but I unfastened my jeans slowly, pulling down the zip until my cock sprang free. Letting it bob in front of me to her rapt gaze, I shoved my jeans over my hips slowly.

My cock twitched, practically sniffing for her pussy and the way home. Precum leaked from the tip in a pearly drop she never looked away from. Slowly, she reached out with a tentative finger and ran the tip through the thick fluid, bringing it to her lips like she was in a trance. Then her eyes closed in bliss and she hummed in pleasure.

I didn't move for a long time, letting her look her fill and touch me however she wanted. Her fingers caressed my cock up and down its length, driving me to madness. Still, I held on. She needed this. To know she could touch me whenever and however she liked. Because I was hers. Same as I'd been telling her she was mine.

When Odette met my gaze, her eyes were glazed over with lust, her lips were parted, and her breath was coming in little pants. I raised an eyebrow and glanced to the condom packet I'd tossed beside her on the bed. She blinked rapidly as if coming out of a trance.

"I-I'm sorry."

"Condom or no, baby. Tell me now or I'm making the decision."

"We probably should…"

"Didn't ask what we should do, Odette. Asked what you wanted to do."

Eyes widening and filling with a kind of panic she shook her head. "You choose."

I nodded and reached for the foil packet. Before I could open it, however, she stayed my fingers with her hand. "No. Wait." She pulled the condom from my hand and tossed it back to the bed. "Why do I want this with you?"

"Because you know you're mine."

Her features hardened and that damned sexy chin went up. "No condom."

I felt the corner of my lips lift. It was a habit I was developing when she did something I wanted. She didn't exactly surrender to me so much as she convinced herself the whole thing was her idea to begin with.

"Be very sure, Odette. I meant what I said. No taking this back."

"Considering we already established the fact that you weren't letting me go anyway, I don't think that's a factor."

I grunted, lowering myself over her again. I positioned my cock at her pussy entrance but didn't enter her. Not yet. I needed that extra few seconds to get a firm hold on my control.

"This first time's gonna be hard and fast, Odette. Later, I'll work on gentle and drawing out your pleasure. When I do that, I might just keep you here for hours riding the edge of your orgasm. Days."

When she gasped out her shock and I felt her pussy twitch against my cockhead, I pressed forward. The second the head entered her I knew I was in trouble. Yeah. This wasn't going to last long. If I made it beyond a couple shallow thrusts, I'd be damned lucky. For a man who prided himself on his control and claimed to lack emotional connections, I was so far gone in a sea of emotions it obliterated my control.

Burying myself to the hilt, I forced myself to stop. Odette screamed, her pussy contracting around me as she came.

"Fuck me," I gasped out as sweat coated my body because of my effort to hold off my own climax. Odette wiggled on my cock, thrusting and twisting her hips in an erotic dance. She might be the best actor in the world, but if her reactions weren't genuine, I couldn't tell it. I might have trouble with people, but Odette I was getting to know. She had this dazed but blissful look on her face as she took her pleasure. Her cheeks were pink and her lips red where she bit down on the bottom one occasionally. She was, in a word, magnificent.

I gripped the tops of her thighs, moving my hips to surge into her with ever increasing strokes. Then I slid my hands up to her hips and waist. Her eyes went wide in a maniacal grin.

"Yes, Cyrus," she breathed. "Fuck me hard!"

With a fierce growl, I bared my teeth. "You don't get to dictate the ride, baby. You're not in charge."

She raised herself up on her elbows, looking down at our joined bodies before reaching one hand between us and stroking her clit. "Yeah?"

Her breathing came faster and faster as she circled her fingers over the sensitive nub twice more. Before I could yank her hand away, she came, her sweet little pussy clamping down on my dick like a vise. I yelled just as she screamed, taking me into a bliss I'd never known existed.

* * *

Odette

What the hell had just come over me? Sex had never been like that. I should have been prepared after the one other encounter I'd had with Cyrus. He hadn't even fucked me then. Now, however, I'd felt like I imagined a nymphomaniac would feel. I was so out of control there was no way I could refrain from taking what I wanted.

And why the fuck had I stopped Cyrus from using a condom? He'd made the choice when I wouldn't, then I'd stopped him. When Steve had done it before, I'd been horrified. Now all I felt was… peace. I knew why. I was now Cyrus's. He'd told me that was the final straw and I'd taken that out. The way out of my old life and into a new one with Cyrus in my life.

"Little witch." Cyrus collapsed over me, his cock still inside me. He kissed my neck and the side of my face before moving to my mouth and gifting me with languid kisses. Like he was praising me for letting him have me.

"Why would you call me that?"

"Because," he said between kisses at my neck, "In all the years I've been sexually active, ain't never been a woman could make me lose control like you just did." He pulled back to smile down at me. It was a lazy, sleepy smile. A well-satisfied smile. "That was the best experience of my fuckin' life, Odette. And it was all you."

For Cyrus, that was akin to poetry, and it made me smile. "For me too." I laid a hand on his face, stroking his beard. I loved the slightly coarse texture, especially when he rubbed it over my chest and nipples. I shivered thinking about it.

He chuckled. "There you go again. Insatiable little witch."

"I never have been before," I muttered. "Maybe you're the one who's bewitched me."

With one last kiss, he pushed off me and off the bed. "I guess it's all just us. Together." He stood there several seconds just looking at me. My legs were still spread, his seed seeping from my pussy, sweat cooling my body. I was self-conscious and felt my face heat up down my neck to my chest, but I didn't close my legs or cover my breasts.

His nostrils flared. "Cup your tits, Odette. Play with your nipples."

I gasped, shocked at the idea. "I'm not doing that." But my hands crept up to do exactly what he said.

When I started to close my thighs, he shook his head. "Don't. Keep your legs spread. Like seeing your pussy filled with my cum."

I groaned and squeezed my breasts. My fingers found my nipples and twisted and tugged to the point of pain. I sucked in a breath as the pain morphed into pleasure as I saw Cyrus's face fill with a dangerous lust.

"That's it, baby. Now stroke your pussy. Let me see my cum on your fingers."

"This is so…"

"Naughty? Sexy?"

"Erotic." The word was a mere whisper of sound. This play had me nearly as wound up as I was earlier.

Without another thought, I did what he asked. I dipped my fingers into my freshly fucked pussy, coming out with creamy cum on my fingers. I spread them apart to watch in fascination as the viscous fluid clung to my skin.

"Clean them off." His growl was sexy as fuck. At first, I wasn't sure what he wanted. I looked around for a tissue or something, but he leaned over me and took my wrist, gently guiding my fingers to my mouth. My eyes widened.

"Never done that before," I whispered even as I opened my mouth. Cyrus let go of my wrist with my fingers hovering at my lips.

I finished the move, putting my fingers in my mouth and closing my lips around them. His seed was slightly salty but not unpleasant. The act seemed dirty, but erotic. Forbidden. Exciting!

I groaned and sat up, then sank to my knees on the floor in front of him, gripping his hip in one hand while taking his cock with the other. He stood there with his hands at his sides, the muscles of his abdomen rippling before my gaze even as his cock hardened and lengthened once again.

With a whimper, I kissed the head of his dick before taking it into my mouth and sucking. I was rewarded with a drop of his cum. I wasn't sure if it was precum or what was left after our earlier encounter, but I was growing addicted.

"Suck me down, Odette," he bit out. "Take me deep."

I tried, but his cock was thick and long. I felt my teeth scrape him and pulled back when he hissed.

"I'm sorry," I said, looking up at him in alarm. I was fucking this up. The most beautiful experience of my life, and I was messing it up because I didn't know how to suck a cock this thick.

"Have you ever sucked a cock before?"

"Only once. But..." What was the etiquette here? "He wasn't nearly as thick. I hurt you."

"No, baby. You didn't. Do what's comfortable if you want to continue. This isn't mandatory."

"NO!" I gripped his hips, glaring up at him. "Mine!"

That got a bark of laughter from him. "Yeah, baby. It's definitely yours."

I enclosed the head in my mouth again, sucking and licking the bulbous head, licking and swirling my tongue over and over. Cyrus let his head fall back and groaned. The muscles of his chest, arms, and shoulders bulged while the veins and tendons in his neck stood out in stark relief. I had never seen anything sexier in my life. Why I hadn't waited for this man to come into my life before giving my virginity to another would forever haunt me. Cyrus had shown me more respect and pleasure than Steve ever had.

Trying to take him deeper, I forced him farther into my mouth until I felt him against my back teeth. It wasn't enough to gag me but was decidedly uncomfortable. My jaw ached, but I didn't want to stop. I wanted to make him lose control again. I wanted... to look into his eyes as he came down my throat and know it had been me to take him there.

I didn't have to wait long before sweat sheened

over his skin and droplets fell from his face to mine. Looking up to his face, I willed him to look at me. To see *me* with my lips around his cock. In a desperate bid to get his attention, I dug my nails into his ass where I gripped and urged him to move.

"Fuck, Odette... *Fuck!*" His nostrils flared, and he bared his teeth at me. "Pull back -- if you don't, my load will go down your throat. Pull back now!"

I didn't. Instead, I gripped him even tighter, keeping my eyes open, looking up at him while he fucked my face with shallow pumps of his hips. Seconds later he roared his release, never taking his gaze from me. Great ropes of cum spurted from his cock into my mouth. I swallowed as fast as I could, not wanting to miss a drop.

"Finger yourself, Odette! Come with me!"

Not doing what he asked wasn't even possible. One hand went to my clit and I stroked. Seconds later, I followed him, screaming around his softening cock as I sucked the last of his cum from him.

The next thing I knew, Cyrus was lifting me into his arms. He carried me to the bathroom, only setting me on my feet to start the shower. Still, he kept one arm around my back, clamping me against his body. Just as well. My legs were Jell-O.

He washed us both, seeming to take delight in simply touching my body. I couldn't deny I enjoyed the feel of his calloused, rough hands on my skin. We didn't talk. Honestly, I wasn't sure I could. For the first time since I found out Steve was essentially leading a double life, my mind was blessedly quiet.

"Sit on the shelf, baby." Cyrus urged me to where he wanted. When I sat, he knelt between my legs with a cloth. I started to close my legs reflexively, but he placed a hand on my knee, meeting my gaze steadily. I sighed and smiled, relaxing as he stroked my thigh. I nodded and he washed between my legs. It was an intensely intimate gesture, one I never expected from anyone.

He washed me carefully, touching me gently. When he finished, I expected he'd help me to my feet. Instead, he leaned in and kissed my mound before his tongue snaked out and lapped at my wet flesh.

"Cyrus! What are you doing?"

"Ain't you had this before?"

"NO!" I tried to push him away, but he was having none of it.

"Be still, baby. Let me taste you. Please."

Cyrus wasn't one to say please. As he'd put it before, he avoided the word *no* at all costs because he hated the word. He could have continued on, and there was no way I'd have stopped him. It was just -- the sensation was so foreign I wasn't sure what to do with it.

In a move that I never thought Cyrus would be capable of when he really wanted something, he didn't take what he wanted until I nodded my consent. He already knew he could have what he wanted from me. The way I'd behaved when we'd had sex was a hard clue. I wanted to take every part of him he wanted to give.

Once I nodded to him, he stroked my lips with his tongue gently, taking a tentative taste before flicking my clit lightly.

"Fucking delicious, Odette. Absolutely fucking delicious." Then he tugged me to the edge of the shelf and buried his face between my thighs. It was just one more thing in a long list I'd been missing from sex. It was then I realized I'd never willingly go back to sex the way I'd had it with Steve. I deserved pleasure. I deserved to be treated the way Cyrus had treated me during our time together.

It didn't take long for him to push me up and over the edge of madness. I cried out a powerful orgasm that had my body seizing up and my back arching. My thighs clamped around his head as I ground my pussy against his lips, trying to ride out waves of pleasure on instinct.

When it was over, when I settled back to earth, I was as drained as I'd ever been. My mind was quiet. My body sated. I have no idea how Cyrus got me dried and into our bed, but the next thing I knew, he was turning out the light and pulling me against him. I rested my head on his chest and he kissed my forehead before stilling himself.

I was floating between sleep and wakefulness, breathing in the masculine, spicy scent that was all Cyrus. Before I realized I was going to say it, the words, "I love you," slipped from my lips. Then I sighed and let sleep have me.

Chapter Eight
Odette

"Wake up, honey." I stretched as Cyrus kissed and nuzzled me awake. There was a sliver of sunlight peeking through the curtains in his room but otherwise, I had no clue as to the time.

"Whassup?"

"We have company coming, honey. Your brother is on the way to meet us here."

I stiffened. "Donovan? Why?"

"You knew I called him to let him know you were here. He's concerned about you. Likely thinks he's bringing you home."

"But he has patients to see. Did you tell him we were together?"

Cyrus snorted. "If I had, I have no doubt the whole of Salvation's Bane would be here instead of Blade alone. No. I thought it best to get you inked and wearing my property patch before I tell him. Still might cause a war between our clubs."

I bit my lip. "I don't want to cause you problems, Cyrus."

"You ain't, baby. Besides, once you're inked, we'll have the whole of Iron Tzars at our backs. Besides, it might take some convincing, but I don't think your brother will kill me too much."

I blinked. "Did you... Did you just make a joke?"

He was silent, looking at me with a blank expression for several seconds. Then he grinned. We both chuckled.

After stretching and protesting appropriately, I walked naked to the bathroom. Soon after that, I found myself facing the vanity while Cyrus railed me from behind. As always, I loved watching the intensity of his expressions. Cyrus might not be able to relate to emotions or understand exactly what he was feeling, but they were there. And, by the look of his face while he did it, the man loved fucking me. I was good with that.

After our morning delight, we met Ace in his shop. The man was covered in all kinds of artistic ink, even up the sides of his neck and into his hair. There were instruments and ink laid out neatly on a table beside the lounge chair, along with a few sketches he'd made in anticipation of our arrival.

"Wylde said this was a rush job," he said to Cyrus with a grin. "You expecting trouble?"

Cyrus shrugged. "Nothing I can't handle."

I rolled my eyes. "My brother is on his way. Cyrus thought it best to get this done before he tries to take me back to Florida."

"Should I be concerned? 'Cause I have no desire to be collateral damage if he doesn't accept his sister being old lady to this asshole."

Cyrus took a threatening step toward Ace, but I twined my fingers through his. "My brother only wants me happy, Ace. He's not going to hurt anyone if I'm happy."

The man glanced from me to Cyrus. "Just out of curiosity, who's your brother? Anyone I know?"

"Donovan Muse," I said with a smile.

Ace actually took a couple steps back. "Wait. Donovan Muse. *The* Donovan Muse. Blade. From Salvation's Bane."

I frowned. "That a problem?"

"Are you fuckin' kiddin' me? His name's Blade, for Christ's sake! I wasn't there, but I heard a guy tell the story of how he got his road name. I have no desire to be the one to give his sister a property tattoo without his knowledge."

"You can be afraid of a man who's not here, or a man who is. Me." Cyrus had a thunderous look on his face. Like he was ready to do murder. It was as alarming as it was charming, in a crazy kind of way. Cyrus saw this as the last barrier keeping me from him. All he had to do was make it happen and I was his.

"I'm afraid of that girl's brother. Ain't too proud to admit it. Isn't she his baby sister? Cause she don't look old enough to be anything but. She even legal?"

"I'm eighteen." I glanced at Cyrus, unsure of the protocol. "Do you need my driver's license?"

"No. Don't need your license." Ace grumbled, scrubbing his hand down his face. "I'm not sure about this, Cyrus. Blade know you're with his sister?"

"He will. When he gets here and sees her ink. Now. You gonna do this the easy way or the hard way?"

Ace and Cyrus stared at each other a long time before Ace backed down. "Fine, you bastard. But this is all on you. I'm not taking responsibility for any of it."

"Good."

We started going over designs and I chose one he'd designed with a colorful hummingbird holding a red heart dangling from a thread. Above it in elegant script were the words, "Property of" and below it woven into the branch the bird was perched on "Cyrus."

"It's so lovely," I said, my fingers lightly grazing the design. "But I have a question before we begin."

"Ask anything you like. I want you sure and confident of everything before we start."

"I'm close to seven weeks pregnant. It's safe to do this. Right?"

I looked at Cyrus, who looked startled, then to

Ace who was shaking his head with a look of utter relief on his face.

"Thank fuckin' God! No. It's not exactly dangerous, especially here, but I'm sure the Surgeon General recommends against it." He gave Cyrus a triumphant look.

"I'll get Stitches' opinion. I don't want to put the baby at risk, but I really want this done."

"I'll do whatever you think is best, Cyrus. You've earned my trust." It surprised me how true those words were. I did trust Cyrus to make decisions like this for me. I knew that, if there was any danger and he chose to go ahead with this, the benefits of having his ink on me outweighed the risks. And it would have to be a huge gap.

He fired off a text to Stitches. It wasn't long before he got a reply. He must not have liked what he read because his scowl deepened. "Mother fuck. Can nothing go right today?" His complaint was muttered as he scrubbed a hand behind his neck. "I need an alternative, Ace."

"What about henna? It's not permanent and would have to be touched up at least once a week until we can get her inked. There won't be much color other than a reddish brown, but it could mark her until it's safe."

Cyrus looked at me. "What do you think?"

"I'll do whatever you want me to, Cyrus. I know you won't lead me wrong."

He shot off another text, looking a little more settled after my words. Seconds later, he got a reply.

"Stitches says the henna is safe. I'll have to talk to Sting and Brick about it. See what they recommend since we can't get you inked properly. I'll present this as our alternative."

"I'm sure he'll have to put it to a club vote," Ace said. "Shoulda been done a while ago, but we never considered there'd be a need." He shook his head. "I'll do the henna, Cyrus, but not the real tatt until after she delivers."

"Not perfect, but it's the only option we've got. I won't put the baby at risk."

I sucked in a breath. "Like I did." My voice was soft and guilt rode me once again. I'd struggled with it since the day I'd woke up so sick after my night of feeling sorry for myself.

"Honey, it was one time. And you only suspected you were pregnant. Given the circumstances, I think you needed a break from reality. We're taking care of you and the baby now. Everything will be fine."

"I hope so."

Cyrus squeezed my hand and smiled. "Worry about how to keep yourself healthy from this point forward, lil' bit. We'll worry about anything else if it becomes an issue."

The next couple of hours was done in subdued silence. Ace spoke softly when he had questions while Cyrus stood next to me, holding my hand while Ace worked. He did a single-color variation of my hummingbird. The design was the same, though. Once he'd finished with me, he worked on Cyrus. His tattoo was my name in the same elegant script inked around his ring finger. Cyrus had him add "Beloved Mate" along the inner side of his finger. Naturally, that set off a bout of crying on my part.

"Stupid hormones," I sniffed before Cyrus dried my tears and gave me a tissue to blow my nose.

He kissed me gently. "Lean on me, Odette. Cry if you need to. I'll keep you safe."

"I know you will." I gave him a watery smile. Then we left Ace's place and went to see Sting.

"We'll have to discuss it in church, but what alternative do we have? It's just bad timing, and we'd never insist either of you willingly put the baby at risk. Not unless it's life or death. This can wait. The temporary tattoo will do for the short term." He shrugged. "It might be necessary to restrict her movements within the club without an escort until she's fully inked, but as long as you're with her, Cyrus, everything will be fine."

"She's not going to be more loyal after she's inked than she is now. But rules are rules."

"Once we discuss it in church, I'm sure we'll come up with a reasonable plan for her to exist with us inside the compound as an old lady to you."

"Seems like all I do is cause problems."

"You're not a problem, Odette," Cyrus assured. "We're in uncharted territory. At worst, you'll be confined to the areas the other families are unless you have an escort. No one's going to consider you a problem."

"We're having to adapt is all," Sting offered. "We've been doing it a lot in the last few months. Not the first time. I'm sure it won't be the last."

While we sat in the common room chatting, the door opened and my brother strolled in, his gaze darting around the room. When he found me, he let out a harsh breath.

"Odette. Thank God you're safe." He hurried to me, pulling me into his embrace when I stood. "Why'd you take off? You had me worried sick."

"There's been some things going on in my life I didn't tell you about. Everything kind of came to a head, and I just needed to get away."

"All the way from Palm Beach to Evansville? Honey, that's a thousand miles! What happened that you ran a thousand miles away?"

I glanced at Cyrus who was standing by my side. I was so nervous I thought I might throw up. Knowing my brother was on the way and him standing in front of me were two entirely different things. My brother loved me with everything he was. He'd taken care of me when our parents had died and had done it gladly. He'd never made me feel like I was in the way or a responsibility he didn't want. He'd loved me and given me everything he could emotionally as well as materially.

Taking a shaking breath, I blurted it out. "Donovan, I'm pregnant." I gripped Cyrus's hand as hard as I could, terrified of my brother's reaction. What I got wasn't what I was expecting.

Donovan jerked like I'd struck him, then blinked rapidly. He glanced down at mine and Cyrus's laced fingers then to me. Then to Cyrus. Before I knew what was happening, Donovan lunged at Cyrus and landed a haymaker across his jaw.

"You son of a bitch!"

"Donovan! Stop!"

"You better do the right thing and take care of her if she's carryin' your kid, you bastard. You don't? You'll find out why they call me Blade."

Cyrus had let go of my hand right before Donovan landed his punch. He staggered backward two steps from the impact but stayed on his feet.

"Donovan! It wasn't Cyrus! He's been nothing but good to me since I got here! Please stop!"

I thrust myself between Donovan and Cyrus, putting my hands on my brother's chest to hold him back. He glanced down at me, then did a double take.

Then his gaze locked on to the henna tattoo on my right inner forearm. If anything, the sight enraged him more. He snatched my wrist and turned my arm so he could examine it.

"That's not a real tattoo."

"No," I said. "It's henna. Stitches said it wasn't safe for me to get the real one until after I have the baby."

"This is a property patch, Odette. Do you know what that means?" Donovan was angry as hell, that was obvious. He tried to calm himself when talking to me, but it was easy to see he was losing what little patience he had left.

"Yes. I know."

"And you're good with being Cyrus's woman? His old lady?"

"Yes, Donovan. I am."

Donovan turned his gaze on Cyrus. "I don't like this, Odette. I think you should come back with me to Palm Springs and let me take care of you. We'll find a man in Bane to be your protector. Someone I trust."

Cyrus stepped closer to me and gently pulled me away from my brother and urged me to the side. "She's mine, Blade. I think she has been since the night I carried her to you after that prospect snuck her in the Bane compound. I just didn't realize it."

"What if I tell you I forbid this? You going to go against me and marry my sister anyway? What if I told you you're not nearly good enough for her?"

Cyrus looked confused. He glanced at me before speaking slowly, like he was trying to choose his words carefully. "You're OK with me banging your baby sister without making her my wife?"

I groaned at the same time Blade struck out again. This time, he launched himself at Cyrus. The two men tussled on the floor, each struggling to get the upper hand. Cyrus gave as good as he got but didn't seem out for blood. Donovan, on the other hand, was doing everything he could to hurt Cyrus. I had no doubt that, had Cyrus been less of a fighter, Donovan would have seriously hurt him. But, honestly, what did Cyrus expect when he phrased that question the way he had? What the hell was he thinking? He was asking for the beating he was currently getting.

"You fucking bastard! I'm gonna kill you, you sumbitch!"

"I told you," Cyrus grunted. "She's mine." Another grunt. "What did you think I meant?"

"She's gonna be your old lady, Cyrus. You're gonna be faithful." Punch. Grunt. "You're gonna take care of her." More grunting. "And you're Goddamned well gonna marry her and give her, as well as this baby, your name! You don't, you'll answer to me, Goddamnit!" Donvan had his arm over Cyrus's throat, bearing down with all his weight. Why Cyrus wasn't fighting back was anyone's guess. Looking at him while my brother was trying to beat the shit out of him, there was no sign Cyrus thought he was in a fight for his life. Sure, he looked like he was exerting himself, but there was no fear or concern about him whatsoever.

"So, you're saying," Cyrus gasped out, "I have your permission," another gasp, "to marry your sister?"

"No! I'm sayin' you *better* fuckin' marry her if you know what's fuckin' good for you!"

The second the words were out of Donovan's mouth, he froze, a look of horror on his face. It took me a second, but I realized what Cyrus had just done. He'd played my brother perfectly. The superior grin on

Cyrus's face said it had all gone according to plan.

Donovan collapsed back on his ass on the floor, then started chuckling. "You son of a fuckin' bitch. Fuck."

"Makin' new friends, Cyrus?" Wylde popped his head out of his office, a wide grin on his face. "This is just one of many reasons I'm glad I brought you to that bar the other week." He waved his hand in Donovan's general direction. "You need friends in your life, man. I made it my mission to see to it you had all kinds of friends."

"You're one step away from getting your *Fortnite* account deleted, Wylde," Sting threatened.

Wylde's shit-eating grin faded to one of utter sadness. Like he was a kid with a new toy a mean adult had decided he couldn't have. Too bad he spoiled the effect by winking at me.

"Fixin' to put that eye out, Wylde." Cyrus's threat was casual. He might have been talking about the weather while he sat in the floor on his ass. He wiggled his jaw from side to side where my brother had connected more than once.

"Man. You guys are takin' away all my fun today." Wylde leaned against the door frame to his office and blew a bubble with the gum he chewed. Then he grinned again, obviously not intimidated in any way.

Cyrus got to his feet and reached out to my brother. Donovan looked at his hand for several seconds before taking it and letting Cyrus help him to his feet. "Gonna have to keep an eye on that one, Odette. He's slippery."

I grinned. "He is. But he's wonderful, Donovan. He's been really good to me."

"I take it you're learning how he works? He's a

little difficult to take sometimes."

"We've had some bumps in the road, but I know he cares for me."

Donovan's features hardened again as he snapped his gaze to Cyrus. "You *care* for her."

Cyrus didn't flinch. "I do. Very much."

"Do you love her?" Donovan raised an eyebrow. I could see the anger simmering beneath the surface of his civility. He'd calmed down, but the potential for this to go back to blows was still there.

There was a long silence. Cyrus's face was a hard mask now as he looked at my brother. Now, it was Cyrus who was angry. But why?

"You know I don't deal well with emotions, Blade. You were the one who helped me figure out why my moods were so erratic and anything out of my routine fucked with my head. I could tell you I love her, but I'm not certain I actually know what love is." He shook his head, that first gesture I noticed from him when he was unsure of himself. Like he was having an internal argument and not altogether sure he was winning. "What is love, Blade? You ask me if I love her, but what is it? I've heard people say they love ice cream, or steak. Is that the same as loving a person?"

"You know it's not, Cyrus," Donovan snapped. "Don't fuck with me on this. Do. You. Love. Odette."

Cyrus turned to me. "Odette, I never want to lie to you. Not about anything."

I smiled at him. "You don't have to explain yourself, Cyrus. You show me your feelings with the way you take care of me. You may not get it, but I do. I'd much rather feel your love for me than have you say it."

That must have been the exact right thing to say. Cyrus visibly relaxed, then pulled me into his arms and hugged me tightly.

"Not lettin' you go, lil' bit. Not ever."

"I'm not letting you go either."

"Uh, in case anyone wants to know…" Wylde waved his hand to get our attention. He was still blowing bubbles while he leaned against the door frame. "One Steve Gleeson is on his way here."

"What?" My stomach dropped.

"Yeah. You know the dude's loaded? I extended an invite to see the sights of Evansville, but he declined. Unfortunately, when his limo picked him up at his side piece's house, Clutch was driving. He wasn't too keen on sightseeing on the way here from West Palm Beach. Clutch said he preferred to ride in the trunk where he didn't have to look out the windows."

Chapter Nine
Cyrus

Iron Tzars owned several properties in and around the Evansville area. Or rather, there were properties owned by people who only existed on paper. Wylde was a genius with shit like that. Nothing could be traced back to the club or any of her members or anyone we associated with. Shit happened on those properties sometimes. Several people we'd had to deal with in the barn had ended up there. Usually in a sinkhole or in pieces next to a pig farm where the bodies would never be found. 'Cause they were eaten. You know. By the pigs. Clutch took the esteemed Mr. Gleeson and his fancy-ass limo to one such property. What happened next would depend entirely on that bastard Gleeson.

We pulled up to the copse of trees where Clutch had driven the limo. The road leading to the property was private for several miles in one of the most rural areas of the state. Even though it was nearly impossible anyone saw us drive into the area, none of us were on our bikes. Instead, I drove myself, Odette, and Blade in an old Bronco while Brick and Wylde led the way in an equally old F-150.

"I still may have to kill you, Cyrus," Blade said conversationally. "I'm pretty sure it's in the big brother code of conduct."

"You won't." I wanted to smirk but refrained. I'd gotten one over on Blade and the other man was stewing. He'd get over it. Especially if I could prove to him I could keep Odette happy.

"Don't bet your life on it."

"Is that supposed to be a pun, Blade? 'Cause it's a really shitty one." That shut the bastard up, though I saw him rolling his eyes when I glanced in the rearview mirror.

We all exited the vehicles and stood behind the limo. Odette clung to me, her slight body trembling.

"I don't want to do this," she whispered. "To see Steve."

"I'll take you back to the Bronco." I'd started to urge her back when Clutch popped the trunk. A bound and gagged Gleeson grunted furiously, kicking out with his bound legs and thrashing so hard he fell from the trunk to the ground with a bone-jarring thud.

"Bet that hurt." Wylde grinned as he approached the man with Clutch and helped him to his feet, then untied him and removed his gag.

He was wet with sweat, his sparse hair stuck to his scalp. What was probably an immaculate shirt at one time was soaked through. He sat on the edge of the trunk, taking in great gulps of air.

Gleeson looked around until he spotted Odette. His eyes widened then his features turned furious.

"I should have known you were behind this, you little whore!"

"Whooo!" Wylde, the bastard, looked positively gleeful. "You might wanna rethink the 'tude, bro. These are the people who brought you a thousand miles across the country and no one's the wiser. Though, if you want to continue, by all means! Personally, I hope you choose option number two. They don't let me out much and I'd really like some action."

I felt Odette relax against me. She took a deep breath and turned to face Gleeson. "I had nothing to do with this, Steve."

"No? Why'd you show up at the theater when my wife and kids were with me? It's not like Martha would ever believe you. She never does when bitches come for my money."

"Everything's not about you, Steve. I was there to see a movie I'd been looking forward to for months. If you were so worried about getting caught, perhaps you shouldn't tell women you're cheating with that your wife's dead when she's perfectly healthy." Odette seemed to have found her calm, but a fine shiver still ran through her more than once as she stood next to me. Her hand still bunched in my shirt and she moved closer to me. I put my arm around her and held her close. Fuck this guy anyway.

"That your new fling? He know how you tried to screw me out of a whole pile of money?"

"I never asked you for anything. Not in the two months I thought things were good between us and not when I figured out I was the other woman. I never once took money from you."

"Did she give you the song and dance how she was a virgin?" He was talking to me now. I stood by passively when I really wanted to put a bullet in his Goddamned head. "Have you fucked her yet? Because, let me tell you, if you haven't, it's not really worth the trouble. A real cold fish, that one." He chuckled.

"This just gets better and better." Wylde grinned. This time, he had an apple. He took bite. "Keep goin', Stevie boy. Give 'em what for."

"Wylde, you're on thin ice," Brick said casually. "Don't instigate things."

The bastard actually managed to look innocent. "Me? Instigate? I'd never do such a thing! I'm merely wantin' to see the man who hurt our little Odette pay. If a little blood is spilled, I'm not gonna lose sleep."

Gleeson grinned. But he wasn't looking at Odette. He was looking at me. "I bet she tried to get you to fuck her without a condom, too. She did me. Fortunately, I was smarter than that. Bitch was wanting to get pregnant with my child because she thought I'd have to pay child support. The joke's on her, though. I had a vasectomy." He chuckled. "I still fucked her bare, though. Who am I to disappoint my favorite whore?"

With every word he spoke, Odette jerked like he'd punched her. She shook her head, like she was denying what he said. I wasn't sure which part she didn't like, but I didn't like any of it.

"You rich?" Wylde continued eating his apple.

Gleeson smirked. "Exceedingly."

"Bet you didn't make all that money yourself, though." The smirk on Wylde's face was the look that always made me want to punch him in the balls. When Gleeson's face turned even redder and he looked like he was going to tear Wylde apart with his bare hands, I could relate. The man could seriously get under your skin if you let him. "I only say that because only a dumbshit would provoke that man." He shrugged. "Or any man his size with that exact expression on his face. Looks like he could rip you limb from limb and sleep like a baby tonight."

Brick sighed. "Just so you guys know, it was Sting's idea I bring Wylde. I voted to leave him home."

Clutch snorted. "Now where would be the fun in that?"

"I gotta admit," Blade added. "He certainly makes life more interesting."

"I aim to please."

"You're all going to jail for this! My car has a GPS system in it. My security team will be on us in no time."

Wylde looked confused. "GPS?" He looked at

Clutch. "You stole a car with a fancy-shmancy GPS system?"

Clutch just shrugged. "What can I say? The car looked sweet and I thought it was worth the risk."

"Fucker really is a dumbshit." Surprisingly, that muttered comment came from Blade. "But wait. I suppose that's not a fair assessment since he has no idea who he's dealing with." Blade saluted the guy. "Good luck, pal."

"I don't need luck. I have technology on my side."

"Really." Blade stepped toward Gleeson, advancing on him slowly. "If that's true, why do you suppose no one's here not to rescue you? Had you planned on coming a thousand miles north today?"

For the first time, Gleeson looked unsure. He looked around him like he expected his men to suddenly appear. "What do you mean? They'll come for me."

"They had over fourteen hours to find and follow you. Since you're such an important man, I'm certain they tried to contact you in all that time. They have to know you're missing. Right?"

"They do," he said confidently. "I know they do. I also know they're tracking my limo."

"Well, they would be," Wylde interrupted, "if, you know, I hadn't disabled your entire security network, including the GPS in your car, your phone, your watch, and every other gizmo and gadget you own. In fact, I happen to know your deputy head of security is currently wondering what the fuck happened to you. Your wife, however, could give two shits. Why? 'Cause she's bangin' your chief head of security."

The man looked like his head was about to

explode. If steam could come out of someone's ears, Gleeson would look like a cartoon character. I also had no doubt he'd try to kill Wylde if he could get his hands on him. Unfortunately for Gleeson, Wylde might be a dipshit goofball sometimes, but he was also deadly when he had to be.

"You'll never --"

"Yeah, get away with this. I know." Wylde said with a flip of his wrist. "Heard that at least a dozen times this month. The fact is, it's you who ain't gettin' away with anything." Wylde picked up a manila envelope from the passenger seat of the truck he and Brick rode in. Pulling out a stack of papers, he waved them in front of Gleeson's face. "See this? It's custody papers. You're gonna sign away your rights."

"My rights to what? You're not getting my children, you bastard!"

"Actually, we are. Or, rather, Odette and Cyrus are. She's carrying your baby, and you're not going to protest when Cyrus adopts the child."

Gleeson actually laughed. "Didn't you hear what I said? I had a vasectomy. I can't have kids. The bitch might be pregnant, but it's not mine. And I'm not paying for any bastard child she has."

"Never asked you to," Wylde said with a grin. "One thing you really should have paid attention to when you had that little procedure. Takes at least ten weeks for it to take. Sometimes as long as twelve weeks or more." Wylde asked his next question in a stage whisper. "When'd you get clipped, Stevie boy?"

The man stood there with his mouth open, unable to say a word. Then he shook his head. "No. Not possible."

"Oh, it's not only possible, it's accurate. I had a friend in a lab in a galaxy far, far away do some testing.

We got your DNA from... places. Once the baby's far enough along, we could do a paternity test."

I shook my head. "Not necessary. I believe Odette when she says you're the sperm donor. But it doesn't matter anyway, 'cause you're gonna sign the document Wylde has there whether or not you're the father. That way there are no mistakes."

"Jesus," Wylde muttered as he handed Gleeson a pen. "How can someone so stupid have made so much Goddamned money?" Then he brightened. "Oh, wait! I know the answer to this one! He didn't! It's his wife's money! He just pretends it's his to coax young, vulnerable women to his bed. Then he takes what he wants from them and throws them out like trash. Isn't that right, Stevie boy?" Though Wylde's expression was bright, I could actually see the underlying anger in him. Maybe I was getting better at this whole emotional bullshit.

"Sign the fuckin' papers, Stevie," Brick growled. "I want to get the fuck outta here sometime this century."

"You have to know I'm going to turn you all in to the police when I get out of here, right?"

"And you said I was the dipshit." Wylde shook his head. "Hint. When you've been kidnapped by badasses and taken to one of the most remote areas of a backwater place like Indiana, you don't threaten to turn your captors in to the police when they let you go." He shook his head again, still chuckling. "No wonder your wife's bangin' your security chief. He's gotta be more intelligent than you." He tilted his head, still looking at Gleeson. "Did you ever even find her clit, Stevie boy?"

Gleeson's tirade got cut short before it even started when Brick one-punched him in the head. The man dropped like a stone.

"Brick," Wylde sighed, sounding for all the world like a disappointed parent. "We didn't get the papers signed. You were supposed to wait until he signed the papers."

"Yeah, well, I'd had enough of his blustering and shit. It's not like we care anyway. This was about revenge for our sweet girl, Odette."

"Oh, I got that for her." Wylde's grin was positively gleeful. "In spades. In fact, I'd be willing to bet my left testicle old Stevie boy there would rather get punched in the head again than go through what he's getting ready to go through."

"What did you do?" Odette turned her head where she'd buried it in my chest, and I wanted to growl at Wylde. I wanted her taking comfort in me. Not curious about what Wylde had in store for this bastard.

"He's going to lose everything he has, Odette. Everything. I drained every single bank account he has that's not associated with his wife or kids. He'd been siphoning his wife's money since they got married, so she's not gonna be happy to learn about that. He'd managed to get his name on all but his wife's corporate account for her very successful accounting firm. The house, the cars, their summer home in the Hamptons, all of it, I reverted back to her. As of this afternoon -- which is why we moved now -- he doesn't have a penny to his name."

Odette gasped. "Are you serious?"

"Oh, very." Wylde sobered now. "Not only that, but I contacted his wife a week ago. She and I had a nice little chat. Which is the reason she's banging the security chief. I gave her a divorce. The appropriate paperwork is done, the computer shit is filed. She wanted to go back to her maiden name, so I fixed that too. Woman's sharp. She knew there were things that didn't add up, but she didn't want to rock the boat. We compared notes, and she acknowledged what she already knew. Her husband is a lying, cheating bastard who damn near took everything she had."

"Will she be all right?"

"Odette," I sighed. "You're too compassionate for your own good. That woman will be fine." I didn't want her anymore upset than she already was. I know seeing Gleeson had thrown her. She'd tried to be brave and face him with her chin up, but everything he'd said about her had really shaken her self-confidence.

"No, Cyrus. I think she's even more of a victim than I am. What about her children, Wylde? Won't he try to get custody in order to get child support if she's the breadwinner in the family?"

"Nope. Kids ain't his. She had them from her first marriage. A good man from all accounts. Died in the service a year before she met Stevie boy. The kids are safe and she's rid of that loser. Besides all that, she filed charges against him. There are warrants out for his arrest for all kinds of shit including money laundering and tax evasion. We got everyone involved we could think of. I have protections in place to keep her from being collateral damage and to protect her business, but even if this bastard tries to go after her for money or us for this, he's in so much trouble it will look like he's trying to deflect blame. Besides, we all have airtight alibis and, as you said, she's the victim in his little schemes. No one's going to believe a word he says, *and* when it's all said and done, he's going away for a very fuckin' long time."

"I bet she hates me, and I don't blame her."

"No, honey." Wylde spoke kindly to Odette. Like

he knew how fragile she was. I wanted to yank out every single strand of bright green hair in the ridiculous streak on his head one hair at a time. Just to fuck with him. Because he understood Odette's feelings and concerns, and I wasn't sure I'd ever be able to. "She knows he duped you just like he did her. She's a really nice woman, actually."

"We done here?" I needed to get back to the clubhouse with Odette. I needed to make love to her. It was the only way I knew how to express how much she meant to me. To tell her what she needed to hear that I wasn't sure I could ever say and know in my heart the words were true.

"Yep." Brick and Clutch put Gleeson in the back seat of the limo. "I'll take this asswipe outta here and drop him and the limo off across the river. He can go wherever he wants from there."

"We're heading back," I told Brick. "Got shit to do. Take Blade with you, will ya?"

"Oh, no." Blade took Odette's arm and gently extracted her from my arms. I wanted to protest, but I recognized now wasn't the best time. Odette looked shell-shocked and fighting over her like two dogs with a bone would only distress her more. "I'm going with you. Me and Odette need to talk, and now's the perfect time."

"Don't you think she needs time to process all this or some shit?" On some level I knew that wasn't the right thing to say, but it slipped out before I could stop it. "You can talk to her tomorrow."

"Nope. I think now's the perfect time." He led Odette to the Bronco and helped her inside. I clenched my teeth and flipped Wylde off when he cackled like a fucking loon.

Turned out, Blade was on my side. He spoke

quietly with Odette all the way back to the compound. Yes, she was feeling more than a little fragile, but she kept looking at me any time Blade would ask her a question. They were in the back seat, but she'd meet my gaze in the rearview mirror anytime she was unsure of herself. She already relied on me to help when she needed it. That knowledge made my chest swell with pride.

When we were back at the compound, Blade reached out a hand to me. "You keep taking good care of my sister, Cyrus. Don't know what she sees in you, but I'm convinced she loves you." I took his hand and gave it a firm shake.

"I…" I cleared my throat. "She's a good woman."

Blade, the bastard actually grinned. I suppose if there was another man on earth who got me, it was Blade. "I hear ya." Thing was, he probably did.

I took Odette to my room and stripped her bare before getting undressed myself. We lay down in the bed together, and I pulled her to me so her head rested on my shoulder and my arms were securely around her. She didn't cry but I thought she might be holding it all in.

"You can, you know, tell me your feelings or whatever you need to do right now."

"I don't really know what I'm feeling." Her voice was soft and a little mournful, wrapping around my heart and squeezing uncomfortably.

"That's supposed to be my line." As I hoped, that got a small smile from her. But it wasn't nearly enough.

I let the silence stretch on for a while before I asked my next question. "Did you love him, Odette? Does it bother you to know what's about to happen to him?"

"No. Not at all. Either of those things. I thought I wanted him, but I think I knew from the first time we were intimate he wasn't going to be the man for me. It still hurt when I discovered his secret, but had I not realized I might be pregnant, it would have been a relief. I had a way out without confrontation on my part. I mean, finding out your boyfriend has a wife and kids is confrontation enough."

"True." Then I asked the question that was burning inside me. The question I dreaded asking because it put me in a position to hear the word I hated most in the world. This time, hearing it might tear a hole in me big enough to drive a semi through. "What about me? You're still not leaving me, but do you love me?" She'd said it once but had been exhausted and probably half asleep when she had. I needed to know even if I couldn't give her an answer to the same question.

She stilled, then looked up at me. There was a beautiful, soft smile on her face. "Yeah, Cyrus. I love you. More than I ever thought it possible to love someone. Especially in such a short time." She settled back but didn't stop talking. "I had you built up into a fantasy no one could ever live up to. For two years I thought about you and how I wanted my life to be with you."

Just like that, my world crumbled. She might love me, but it was likely I'd never measure up to what she wanted. "I'll be what you need, Odette. I swear I'll figure it out."

"That's the thing, Cyrus. You surpassed everything I thought I ever wanted. Sure, you're abrupt and gruff, but you're one of the best people I know. And you take care of me. You give me what I need."

The band tightening around my chest eased and I found myself shaking with relief. Of course, Odette noticed and frowned up at me.

"What's wrong?"

"Nothing! I…" God! Feelings should be outlawed. They were confusing and messy and… "I love you."

There was silence while Odette blinked up at me, surprise on her lovely face. Then a slow smile graced her features, and I completely lost my heart in that very instant.

"I love you, too, Cyrus."

I cleared my throat. "Good. I'm glad we got that settled."

She laid her head back on my chest. Then I felt her tremble. It took me several seconds to realize she was trying to hold in a giggle.

"Really, Odette?" I rolled my eyes, though the relief inside me was tremendous. "I tell you something I've never told anyone else in the entire world and you're giggling?"

"I can't help it!" She finally gave up all pretense of trying to hide her laughter and crawled on top of me, straddling my hips and pressing her bare pussy against my rapidly hardening cock. "It's like it took the demons of hell to drag that out of you. It's just three little words." She leaned in and kissed me gently even as she continued to smile.

"Yeah, well, it's three words I've never said because I wasn't sure I ever meant them. I know now I do. But only with you."

She reached between us and guided my cock inside her. "I'm glad that you found the words, Cyrus. But I'm partial to action. Why don't you show me how much you love me."

"Oh, baby. Don't say you didn't ask for this." I gave her a cocky grin, my heart swelling with all the love I felt for this woman.

Then I proceeded to show her. For the rest of the day, and into the night. And it... was... *glorious*!

Marteeka Karland

International bestselling author Marteeka Karland leads a double life as an action romance writer by evening and a semi-domesticated housewife by day. Known for her down-and-dirty MC romances, Marteeka takes pleasure in spinning tales of tenacious, protective heroes and spirited heroines. She staunchly advocates that every character deserves a blissful ending.

Marteeka finds joy in baking, and gardening with her husband. Make sure to visit her website to stay updated with her most recent projects. Don't forget to register for her newsletter which will pepper you with a potpourri of Teeka's beloved recipes, book suggestions, autograph events, and a plethora of interesting tidbits.

Series reading order for Iron Tzars MC

More books by Marteeka Karland

Want more? Find Teeka's Dark Erotica side here: Wanda Violet O.

Bones MC Multiverse
Bones MC
Shadow Demons
Salvation's Bane MC
Black Reign MC
Iron Tzars MC
Grim Road MC
Bones MC Print Duets
Bones MC Audio
Salvation's Bane MC Audio
Iron Tzars MC Audio

Changeling Press E-Books

More Sci-Fi, Fantasy, Paranormal, and BDSM adventures available in e-book format for immediate download at ChangelingPress.com -- Werewolves, Vampires, Dragons, Shapeshifters and more -- Erotic Tales from the edge of your imagination.

What are E-Books?

E-books, or electronic books, are books designed to be read in digital format -- on your desktop or laptop computer, notebook, tablet, Smart Phone, or any electronic e-book reader.

Where can I get Changeling Press E-Books?

Changeling Press e-books are available at ChangelingPress.com, Amazon, Apple Books, Barnes & Noble, and Kobo/Walmart.

ChangelingPress.com

Printed in Great Britain
by Amazon